I0621947

The Free World War

The Free World War

Matthew Frend

COSMIC
EGG
BOOKS

Winchester, UK
Washington, USA

JOHN HUNT PUBLISHING

First published by Cosmic Egg Books, 2019
Cosmic Egg Books is an imprint of John Hunt Publishing Ltd., 3 East St., Alresford,
Hampshire SO24 9EE, UK
office@jhpbooks.net
www.johnhuntpublishing.com
www.cosmicegg-books.com

For distributor details and how to order please visit the 'Ordering' section on our website.

Text copyright: Matthew Frend 2018
Maps Designed by Stephen M. Perrine
Edited by James Hallman – Writeworks
Cover artwork "Hellcat – Lorraine 44" by Pete Ashford
https://www.artstation.com/peteashford

ISBN: 978 1 78904 168 2
978 1 78904 169 9 (ebook)
Library of Congress Control Number: 2018947791

All rights reserved. Except for brief quotations in critical articles or reviews, no part of this
book may be reproduced in any manner without prior written permission from the publishers.

The rights of Matthew Frend as author have been asserted in accordance with the Copyright,
Designs and Patents Act 1988.

A CIP catalogue record for this book is available from the British Library.

Design: Stuart Davies

UK: Printed and bound by CPI Group (UK) Ltd, Croydon, CR0 4YY
US: Printed and bound by Thomson-Shore, 7300 West Joy Road, Dexter, MI 48130

We operate a distinctive and ethical publishing philosophy in
all areas of our business, from our global network of authors to
production and worldwide distribution.

Kursk, Russia
July 5th, 1943

The showers of dirt and calamitous thunder that had rent the air for the past hour stopped abruptly. Lieutenant Valentin Rhuzkoi uncurled from the fetal position, pulled himself up and peered over the lip of his trench. He squinted at the wasteland of craters and ruined emplacements, wrapped in a mangled maze of barbed wire.

"*Oh bozhe moi!*" he muttered, spitting out a mouthful of crud he'd breathed in during the artillery barrage. Glancing around, he wondered if he had any men left.

"Positions!" he yelled, raising his field glasses and scanning the defensive perimeter. Helmets began to bob up from the scorched ground to either side.

A light breeze pushed a veil of thick smoke toward them, the remnants of the barrage's last volley. Gray figures loomed through the mist.

"Three hundred yards! Infantry!" he shouted, still unsure how many of his company had survived. How many dead or injured? How many buried alive by the hundreds of shells that had landed directly on their positions? Then a darker shape caught his attention.

"Jagdpanzer!"

The lumbering tank destroyer coughed. A shockwave of pulverized earth slammed him back to the floor of the trench.

He feared his men might answer, but they were well drilled and held their fire, waiting for the Germans to close in.

None came.

The Panzer grenadiers melted into the ruptured landscape, allowing their armor to advance past them.

Lieutenant Rhuzkoi scrambled up the incline of the collapsing trench, half blinded, and dug around for his Kalashnikov.

Another explosion. He could barely breathe as hot, concussed

1

air was sucked away, replaced by choking dust and smoke. He felt something solid, grasped and pulled, then flung it away. Just a bloody arm.

Shots rang out. The sixty-ton monster kept coming on as his men fired their rifles with futility. A few of them leapt out of their holes and threw firebombs.

They were gunned down as shattered glass and flames smashed uselessly against the steel flanks of the Ferdinand.

A Red Army machine gun opened up. The grenadiers were assaulting in groups, leap-frogging from cover to cover. Rhuzkoi saw one get tangled in wire. Halted only for a second, but he jerked suddenly and then fell limp as machine gun bullets thudded into his torso.

The Ferdinand fired another HE round and the machine gun died. Their anti-tank guns already destroyed by the artillery, the Russians had nothing to fight back with.

Rhuzkoi brought his hands up … two clenched fists of scorched clay.

Enough death. Enough blood on his hands.

"Surrender!" he cried to his men as he rose from his trench.

He raised his arms above his head and his hands emptied, the Russian soil falling back down to lay with his dead comrades.

Now Night her course began, and, over Heaven
Inducing darkness, grateful truce imposed,
And silence on the odious din of war.
John Milton
Paradise Lost

General George S. Patton looked out over a vast frozen white plain from his hilltop vantage and imagined the thousand miles beyond.

A figure as solitary as the windswept landscape, he closed his eyes and his mind traveled across the forests, hills and then the rolling steppes, until it reached Moscow.

He shivered, not against the chill breeze, but from Napoleon's ghost brushing his shoulder, and reminding him of the tragic failure of 1812.

His eyes opened moments later, blazing brightly with a renewed purpose. He would succeed where the Grand Armee and Barbarossa had fallen short. He would take Moscow.

The war-horse was being called to arms once more.

Mojave City
2265 CE

"My love … will you read to me?"
"So am I as the rich, whose blessed key,
Can bring him to his sweet up-locked treasure,
The which he will not every hour survey,
For blunting the fine point of seldom pleasure."
"Sweetheart that's wonderful! Am I your treasure?" Eya asked.

"Yes my heaven, you are a precious jewel," Arjon admitted, his voice bursting with emotion.

Eya gave him that look, "Would you like to play now?"

"Wouldn't you prefer to go out?" Arjon asked.

Locks of candy-apple flame swept around her shoulders as Eya stopped to pick a rose.

"I'm not sure if anyone will be out tonight …" she said, "because of the celebration tomorrow."

"We could go to the Nature Green tonight, have a swim in the lake … and then go into the City tomorrow night for the celebration!" Arjon enthused.

"When will you work?" she asked sweetly.

"Anytime! You know that our time together will always come first."

"Let's wait until tomorrow then … the Green and then to the City!"

As the sun sank into the horizon, their bower adjusted to the approaching night. Hesta, the artificial intelligence that embellished their home and managed the practical and mundane tasks, adjusted the air inside their home so that it took on a balmy comfort. Inconspicuous lighting glowed from behind ferns and other greenery, and the window tinting changed to enhance a view of the sunset.

"As long as you're happy …" Arjon agreed, "… I'll go to my

den and do a little work before dinner."

Eya thought briefly about what she would prefer to do. The candy-apple red suddenly burst into crimson fire, as nano-crystals in her hair responded to her mood.

"Mmmm ... work later ... *play now!*"

Hesta planned the evening meal. She knew what the bower's occupants desired by monitoring biometric sensors, and would time the meal's delivery so that it did not interrupt them. She checked their current locations – Arjon in his den and Eya in her studio. Their serotonin readings indicated recent satiation. She would ensure that a stimulant such as chocolate, which also produced endorphins, was included in the ingredients so that the meal would not be too disappointing.

While the AI cooked, Arjon sat at his cluttered oaken desk. The outline of the dark timber portrayed its natural form, carefully crafted as though it were carved from a still living tree. In his hands, a rare paper copy of an antique document transfixed his attention.

"Hesta, I'm going to need a detailed search of military records circa 1945."

"Data from confirmed sources is available," she replied.

"I'll need all personnel files on the following individuals, plus Military Police records, and also transport logistics records for US Army Signals battalions operating near the Mannheim area of Germany in December 1945."

He pressed a spot on the display in front of him and Hesta went to work.

"Once you have all of that, I want you to build a local data matrix – I'll want to do some data-mining on it."

"Understood. The data matrix is estimated to be two petabytes and will be completed within fifteen minutes."

"Great, that seems fast! Is that because of your latest upgrade? The client should be pleased – I'm charging their attorney by the hour and I got the impression they are on a budget."

"Confirmed."

He pondered for a moment while Hesta began processing. Being a lawyer must have been very laborious in the past. Weeks or even months of leg-work and trawling through documents to put together a case. Now his artificial assistant could do all of that, he just needed to provide direction.

And what a different world it must have been in the twentieth century.

He smiled as he imagined the kind of work he would have been doing in the previous centuries.

Defending criminals, settling civil disputes … Qwerty … so much work for the legal profession.

In a world of all-pervasive harmony, his role had evolved into one where the scant demand for his talents lay not in the resolution of conflicts, or recovery of material wealth, but more in the uncovering of the truth – and the restoration of personal honor.

He walked from his den and across to Eya's studio. She was concentrating on her work, a photon-sculpture, and wasn't aware of his presence. He stood and watched her for a moment as she deftly manipulated light emitting plasma into an ultra-modern abstract form. It reminded him of a hologram of a stellar nursery he'd once seen. Swirling bands of color were being drawn into a burning core where a new star would be born.

He had to drag his gaze away as he continued into the room. "Beautiful!"

She giggled appreciatively; "Have you finished already?"

"Soon. I've got a hunch this one would have taken a while if not for Hesta's upgrades – they've improved her virtualization performance."

She broke herself away from her work and embraced him.

"But you're not going to let it change our plans for tomorrow?" she cooed.

"No, no, no … and the whole team's confirmed. It shows we all must think alike."

"So it's an important announcement then?" she asked, curious as to why all of his co-workers would also be going.

Arjon sighed, *artists …* he thought, *in a world of their own most of the time.* But he found it refreshing that his wife could be so detached from an event that his colleagues had been speculating about for weeks.

"*Very* important. It's a new Enlightenment."

"Really!"

"Yes … it's been over fifty years since one was ratified."

She moved back to her sculpture, "That long? We must be running out of ideas that are in need of being proven … *right.*"

As soon as she said them she felt uncomfortable with her words. She looked up at Arjon, "I mean …"

"I know what you mean …" Arjon smiled. "It's not as though we know everything there is to know about our existence. And you're right – the Center of Truth sometimes establishes a concept as being *wrong.*"

Eya smiled warmly at him, appreciating how they could talk easily about anything – even something as controversial as the CoT. There had been spirited dinner party conversations around the civic entity that was entrusted with the verification – and protection, of the truths that by their nature may not be self-evident.

"You know I don't always feel comfortable talking about them … they're so secretive."

"Yes – I know … I sometimes feel the same – but I think it needs to be that way. It seems as though they do what they need to do better without external distractions, or interference. The last couple of hundred years of a CoT without any issues or controversies confirms it."

He watched her work at her sculpting for a moment, the light playing over her shapely figure. She was everything he could ever want.

Talented, interesting, pleasing to his eye … perfect.

He left, feeling gratified that his wife could always lift his spirits and help him to not take the world too seriously.

∞

St. Querin, Germany
July 1945

Valentin Rhuzkoi was still looking around the great hall of the villa in Bad Tolz. He could have been in the country retreat of royalty for all the opulent history lining the walls. Portraits of noblemen on horseback, many in military uniform, were interspersed between vintage weaponry, sabers, cutlasses and several muskets. His inspection had relieved the boredom. He'd been waiting for over an hour.

The clack of hooves on cobblestone alerted him to his host's return. The aide who'd brought him coffee mentioned they'd been on a hunt since early morning. His stomach told him it was good timing, perhaps there would be some lunch before too long. If the surroundings were an indication of the fare, then he should look forward to a significantly better menu than the army diet that he was used to getting.

He walked over to one of the room's many floor-to-ceiling windows and caught a glimpse of a long white tail disappearing into the stable block. It swished impatiently, probably in anticipation of lunch.

Presently, the ornate doors swung open and three men entered. Colonel Blackett he knew, as it was he who had arranged for his very covert arrival at the villa.

General Patton he did not. The general paused at a table to take up and light a cigar. Blackett and the other officer, a Major General, continued on and made the introductions.

"Major General Harker, this is Major Rhuzkoi of the Russian Liberation Army," said Blackett.

They shook hands, then, the Russian offered his palm to General Patton. As the General took it firmly, his blue eyes drilled coldly, leaving Rhuzkoi in no doubt that he was being analyzed, and critically. The Major couldn't help but compare the stern grip to Stalin's which was notably weaker.

"What's your function Major?" Patton asked brusquely.

"I am Liaison Officer to General Andrey Vlasov's Headquarters – Committee for the Liberation of the Peoples of Russia," Rhuzkoi replied curtly.

They sat in a circle of high backed chairs as Colonel Blackett began, "The Major has confirmation from General Vlasov that our plan should proceed with only one minor change."

Patton eyed the Russian officer warily. "I hope it's only minor."

Rhuzkoi nodded. "Yes General, we are confident that it will not affect the outcome of the operation."

"Well then ... spill it as briefly as possible if you will, and then we can get some lunch brought in."

The Major's reaction at the mention of lunch looked a little pained, and the Americans mistook it to mean his forthcoming conditions could be serious.

Although used to the manner of men in power, having served as an interpreter in the Kremlin, Rhuzkoi shifted nervously in his seat. General Patton was different to politicians – the authority was tempered from the heat of battle, not the debating room.

"*Da*, you see ..." he sputtered, "... it is the *duration* of hostilities ... we wish to limit them – in order to reduce our casualties."

He opened his palms pleadingly. "Our Army fought vicious campaigns against Red Army, and then against Nazis ..."

"Yes, yes Major!" Patton insisted, "... we're all aware of the RLA's exploits."

He looked on indifferently, as though he'd read more impressive histories than those described by the reports of General Vlasov's command. The former Red Army General had defected after being captured by the Germans, and his RLA had then fought alongside them against the Soviets. After mistreatment by Hitler, they had then turned against the Germans at the war's end.

Patton's indifference poured ice over any previous cordiality.

"This operation will be conducted with the same unrestrained execution that it would be if it began under any other circumstances."

"Of course General, we just ..." Rhuzkoi's voice tapered away, and he looked to the other two officers for a reprieve.

General Patton continued emphatically, "We don't give a damn about how long it takes Major, but it is going to achieve what it is intended to do ... and goddamned well better *look* good while it does!"

The Russian looked to Colonel Blackett.

The OSS man took a deep breath and looked at Patton, "General, if we assure General Vlasov that we can minimize their potential casualties ... perhaps by accepting their surrender sooner than we'd originally planned ... there shouldn't be any impact on the overall picture."

Patton drew on his cigar and signaled to Harker, his Chief of Staff, that a drink may now be in order.

"I'm sure you gentlemen remember when you came to me with this scheme – I explained that it will only work if it looks authentic. That no one can possibly question its credibility."

Blackett still felt obligated to advocate on behalf of the Russian RLA officer.

"Nobody here doubts the importance of secrecy around this. Only Vlasov himself and his most trusted staff officers have any idea what they are about to start."

Patton took his bourbon from Harker, "And once it starts, nothing but total capitulation will end it – I'll see to that."

"Yes General ..." agreed Blackett, "... once the conflict begins, and then spreads, the identity of those who initiated it will be easy to obscure amongst the chaos that follows. The whole frontier is on a knife-edge. We're getting more reports of Soviet patrols infiltrating our occupation zones every week."

"Convenient ... they may even do your work for you," Patton said to Rhuzkoi.

"As the incursions are into all of the Allied zones, would it be more effective if the French or British were attacked first?" asked Blackett.

"But Colonel," said Rhuzkoi, "then there could not be guarantee that our forces would avoid being eliminated by an army other than your own."

Patton's expression said everything.

So? You're a soldier willing to die for a cause, aren't you?

Harker interjected, "Fair point Major, in addition, we cannot know whether the British or French are capable of putting up a convincing fight. I doubt they have the political will to do anything other than try to negotiate a quick peace, after what they've been through."

"No ... you're probably right ..." Blackett conceded. "... and they won't have the military build-up we're going to have."

Patton viewed Rhuzkoi through eyes that had seen first-hand the devastation of two world wars. He was also a believer in his own destiny – and that his destiny served a greater purpose than any individual part he would play in world events. He wanted to make sure the other players were going to follow the same game plan.

"Colonel Blackett explained to me that your RLA will be fighting against Stalin. To free your people from Bolshevik tyranny."

The Major returned Patton's gaze with a look haunted by decades of murderous oppression against his own people. Millions cast aside to starve in the name of collectivism, or purged at the hands of an ideology which put the State above its own people.

Patton softened his tone. "If General Vlasov wants to save his country, then he knows there'll be a cost."

The bourbon was doing its work, freeing the daily pressures, and loosening the grip that ordinarily suppresses the imagination of such a far-sighted visionary.

"Gentlemen, there can be no constraints that jeopardize the outcome."

He looked beyond his colleagues and through the window to the distance. "I believe the world will be in a much worse state for the generations to come, if we do not succeed in our endeavor."

∞

Cherish therefore the spirit of our people, and keep alive their attention. Do not be too severe upon their errors, but reclaim them by enlightening them.

Thomas Jefferson

The Great Hall reverberated with the excited hum of the gathered crowd. Many thousands had converged on the city for what was sure to be an historic event. Arjon and Eya stood among a group of their friends and colleagues. The day had been full of speculation. What would the Enlightenment be? An extra-terrestrial civilization discovered? The timing of the end of the universe confirmed? Although the suspense was becoming almost unbearable for Eya, she and everyone else's spirits were high.

"So *how* can you know?" She nearly screamed at Margeaux.

"Yes!" Arjon joined in. "This has been the best kept secret since they found life on Europa!"

Margeaux could barely restrain herself, "*Oooohhh*! It's been torture to keep it to myself!" She clutched her partner Grillon's hand tightly, as if she could draw the strength to resist letting it all out. "I can't tell you anything – except ..." and she looked at Grillon for approval. He nodded reluctantly, so she quickly whispered, "*My office ... we were assigned the processing of the legal documents that were finally submitted to the Protectorate!*"

"Really?" Arjon felt as though he'd been scolded. "A legal firm? I would have thought all that went through the Protectorate's own administration."

Grillon spoke up, driven by a compulsion to keep Margeaux from saying too much. "Yes, you're right, that's been the case in the past. The last Enlightenment as you know, was sourced from the academic institutions whose research had proven the existence of gravitons."

"So why the legal involvement with this one?" Arjon demanded. His work in Genealogical Litigation seemed insignificant in light of his friends' revelation. He looked sheepishly at them, suddenly aware of his impatient tone.

"Why … I'm afraid I can't reveal that without breaching disclosure." Margeaux said with palpable discomfort, "You all know how impossibly secretive and remote the CoT are … I've never even spoken to one of them in person!"

No one responded – they all knew the reason for the CoT's remoteness, and why the secrecy around Enlightenments was paramount. History was replete with instances of documented events being tampered with, and the truth distorted, for the self-perpetuating purposes of powerful entities such as monarchies, governments – even churches.

The Center of Truth was independent of all external influences. The people knew the truth when they heard it.

Eya glanced up at one of the stadium screens. "Well, we won't have to wait long to find out what this is all about."

The main lighting dimmed, as illumination from above signaled the start of proceedings. Four thin columns of light descended around the perimeter, and began to increase in size and intensity. Four columns representing the Four Pillars of Society. They soon became too bright to look at. All eyes were averted, and then closed, as the brilliance became so radiant, so intense, that it would penetrate a closed mind.

The Light of Truth.

Moments later, the brightness of the columns diminished suddenly and they materialized into spectacular pillars of transparent crystal.

The Reification. The solidification of the Light – the symbolic opening of a Special Session of the Protectorate.

"How do they do that?" whispered Eya, not wanting to disturb the quiet awe of the crowd around them.

"I don't know … perhaps it's something to do with lasers interacting with the air molecules … but like water freezing into a solid."

"Shhhh!" someone hissed from behind.

Around the world, in auditoriums exactly the same as this one, millions were watching.

The Orator appeared.

Wearing the black and white cloak of his office, he was the spokesperson for the Protectorate, the governing body of the Center of Truth. Those who verified, and then preserved the highest ideals and lexica, the scientific and spiritual knowledge, for all of humanity.

"People of the Free World!"

He paused, allowing the immensity of his words being broadcast around the planet to float in the air for a moment.

"This day will be remembered with the same reverence as all of those days that have changed the course of our history!"

He waited for the cheering and applause to die down. "Many decades of endeavor and experiment have finally borne fruit, and the human race is entering a new era – a renaissance of the spirit!"

Eya and Arjon tore themselves from the spectacle and looked at each other, laughing, as they were caught up in the building excitement.

Above the platform, an enormous holographic image of the Orator changed focus, zooming in on his astute features.

"The Protectorate of the Center of Truth, in its capacity as defender of human integrity, declares …"

Eya held her breath, oblivious to her red hair fading as though being drained of blood.

The Orator raised his arms, "The human soul has been

scientifically proven to exist!"

∞

St. Querin, Germany
July 1945

"You ride well Major," General Patton observed. "Do you have any Cossack in your family tree?"

"No General. I was fortunate enough to spend some years on a farm outside Kiev."

Major Rhuzkoi patted his mount, a Lipizzaner mare, on the wither. "But they were cart-horses compared to this magnificent warmblood!"

"That she is, but goddammit what a waste!" Patton lamented, "Spending years being trained to do gymnastics in a barn, when they could be out here as they were intended to be – galloping through forests and over jumps."

Rhuzkoi cast his eye over the countryside. Patches of fog still blanketed the gullies between low hills, sheltered from the mid-morning sun by the multitude of dark tree-tops.

"*Da! Da!* I agree completely!" he said, relishing his host's perspective and feeling invigorated by the crisp, country air. He urged his mare on into a canter, lining her up on a fallen tree. The great mare leapt over it with graceful ease, and as Patton watched, he was compelled to exceed the effort.

He spurred his stallion on, collecting him up expertly just before the jump, so that rider and horse arced over the huge log with a yard of clearance.

"*Oh Bozhe moi!*" exclaimed Rhuzkoi, "you should be in show-jumping competition!"

They continued at a relaxed walk, eventually coming to a dirt road cutting through a part of the forest that, due to its remoteness, had remained undisturbed since the end of the war two months ago. The road ran atop an embankment, rising several feet above the surrounding forest floor which flooded each spring.

Their horses clambered up the bank, then stopped. Their relaxation was replaced by a tense wariness of the scene before them. The two riders were also taken aback by the sight that beheld them. The aftermath of an airstrike on a Wehrmacht column littered the other side of the road.

"Poor devils" said Rhuzkoi, "... must have been strafed by allied fighters."

In amongst the twisted wreckage of half-tracks and transports full of dead Panzer Grenadiers, were the partially decomposed, now frozen bodies of dozens of civilians strewn amongst their pathetic little carts.

"Allied fighter *bombers*," Patton corrected him, pointing to a bomb crater with his cane.

"This is almost as wasteful as these fine horses not achieving their potential."

Rhuzkoi merely nodded. He understood that Patton wasn't referring to the overall waste of lives, but to the fine soldiery laying on the field. Decimated before they could fire a shot.

It was a soldier's perspective. It wasn't that remorse for the loss of innocent lives wasn't felt, it was still there. However, after years of battling through cities and towns, seeing countless such incidents, a soldier naturally placed a greater value on those in uniform than for any other.

They trotted along the road and soon dismissed the carnage left behind. Both warriors had seen enough destruction for it not to gouge any new scars in their memory.

"Major, what can you tell me about Kursk?"

"Why ... yes, there is much to tell."

"Good. Of course, I've researched the Nazi experience – from captured reports and other intelligence, but I'm hoping you can confirm or elaborate on that."

"Naturally I shall do this."

The Russian considered his words carefully, mindful of the precarious position he and his comrades in the Russian Liberation Army were in. For all he knew he may be about to divulge information of a strategic nature. Information that may assist the Americans to not only defeat Stalin, but bring about the total capitulation of all Soviet armies. General Vlasov's instructions had been clear – to only provide what was required to initiate a war. A war intended to bring about Stalin's downfall – and the end of Bolshevism.

"I must point out that I may only have intelligence that is of little use to you. Although I fought with the Red Army for two years before I was captured, that was two years ago – the data you have from the Germans may be more recent, and of more relevance."

General Patton cut him short, "Allow me to be the judge of that Major. And since you've brought it up ... just how did you come to be an officer serving under a rogue general?"

Rhuzkoi never responded to jibes with a courteous smile. He never smiled. His facial muscles were set to a squared, cold indifference. He sighed, "I was serving as a Lieutenant in the 348th Rifle Division at the battle of Kursk in 1943. We were encircled by an armored division on July 10th, then overrun and taken prisoner. His expression was pained at the memory of the savage conflict. Their weapons useless against the German heavy tanks, and their own T34s knocked out with impunity.

"I was in a POW camp when General Vlasov visited, recruiting for the RLA. He was already taking opportunity of war with Nazis to undermine Kremlin. With my own experience of horrors of collectivism in the Ukraine, I did not need convincing that Stalin was the real enemy of the Russian people."

His eyes lit up and he boasted, "There were over one hundred thousand of us!"

"And after you joined Vlasov, you fought against your own

countrymen?" Patton prompted.

"*Da* ..." again the pain showed, but this time from a place where a deeper guilt emerged. Those they fought and killed would have been their friends or neighbors ... even brothers.

Talking to the General was difficult He could sense he was under intense scrutiny, his honor being questioned, but he had to continue, he was here to build trust.

"At the Oder River in 1945 ... it was January ... very cold. As the Red Army attacked toward Berlin, our 1ˢᵗ Division made a stand alongside the Germans. We were beaten back and retreated toward Prague."

Compassion welled up in the US General. Patton couldn't help but admire Rhuzkoi's conviction. While others may have seen him as a traitor to his country, it was plain to see that his intentions were to right the wrongs of a corrupt regime.

"You're a very brave man Valentin." he said quietly, in tune with the slow rhythmic walk of his horse.

"It takes guts to stand up for your ideals, and then take action to defend them." Patton chuckled softly, "Why hell, you might have been right at home in the American Revolution!"

They continued on for several minutes without speaking. The only sound to disrupt the silent forest, the steady footfalls of the horses. Then the General got back to the subject of the tank battle at Kursk.

"Major, I'm particularly interested in the disposition of the Red Army heavy armor ... and how the SUs and IS tank destroyers were integrated with the main battle tanks."

The Major knew he could not jeopardize his mission by mistrusting the Americans. He proceeded to paint an accurate picture of the sheer, massive volume of Soviet forces at the Kursk salient. Within a one hundred and twenty mile front, over 1.3 million men, 3000 tanks and 20,000 pieces of artillery, arranged in a twenty-five mile deep system of main defenses. Within this area, they had prepared 10,000 miles of trenches and minefields, interspersed with countless bunkers, and anti-tank and machine gun positions.

Against this immense defensive system, the Nazis had thrown more divisions and aircraft than they had amassed for the invasion of Russia two years earlier.

Rhuzkoi also described how close the Germans had come to defeating his countrymen. Only a lack of resources such as fuel, and an insufficient number of divisions in reserve, had caused them to fall tragically short.

"Their heavy armor, in particular the Tiger tanks, were at times unstoppable. The guns of T-34s were useless against them. Some commanders even resorted to ramming the enemy giants."

Patton thanked the Major for his account. It confirmed his own data, but he'd needed to hear it from Rhuzkoi himself. In the current post-war climate, trust was a valuable commodity.

His mind furiously processing the information, the general reinforced his ideas of the Red Army's vulnerabilities. In his description of the battle, the major had described a kind of "mobile attrition" where armored units had continually destroyed each other in the fighting around key positions. Both sides incurred extremely high losses, and only the side with the most numerous resources could withstand them for a prolonged period. General Patton made a mental note on how to address this tactic with a plan he'd recently heard from one of his junior staff officers regarding the use of tank destroyers.

Lost in their own thoughts, the two made their way back to the villa where Colonel Blackett awaited them.

∞

And ye that live and move, fair creatures, tell,
Tell, if ye saw, how I came thus, how here?
John Milton
Paradise Lost

The Great Hall
Mojave City
2265 CE

"The soul ... *proven!*"

The crowd suddenly hushed. Exasperated faces looked at each other, searching for a way to express what this new understanding would mean to them. No one had expected this. In the days leading up to the event, speculation had been rife that the announcement would be about the discovery of an extra-terrestrial civilization.

Arjon saw Margeaux's face brighten, absolved of the burden she'd been carrying. Then it dawned on him, *Of course!* He turned to Eya and explained, "The law ... imagine the ramifications!"

Eya's mind, still grasping at the announcements ballooning possibilities ... came back to earth with a thud. "Laws? Hey what about the *important* things ... like death? Or the lack of it? Does this mean we're eternal?"

Arjon laughed, as much at himself and his mortal viewpoint, as at his spouse's joyful, if slightly fantastic speculation.

They turned their attention back to the Orator.

"The details of the founding research will be made available to the communication network shortly. For now, you must also be aware of an addendum to the decree ... that the Free World will enact in all member countries, civilian legislation that will acknowledge, and by apropos, defend, the rights of a new legal entity – hereby known as the Human Spirit."

Arjon chuckled, his mind spinning and weaving a framework of new possibilities. Not just for the way of life for all people – but also for his own career.

"Qwerty!" "This is literally going to change the world!"

They left the Hall to join the celebrations beginning in the streets outside. Pyrotechnic displays lit up the entire sky, the like of which had never been seen before. Light and sound rained down from high up in the atmosphere, providing a backdrop for the party which would last long into the night.

The celebrations continued over the next several days. Arjon and Eya hosted friends, enjoying the reveries over dinner.

"Just think …" Arjon mused, "I now have rights and legal consideration … above those limited to my physical form!"

Eya took a sip of champagne. The endless hours of conversation and exploring new ideas had been thrilling, but she was longing to return to her workshop and expend some of her pent-up creativity. She knew that newly charged inspiration would flow into her artwork as a torrent.

Arjon's words called her back to the table.

"A new born child … innocent and untainted by the world they are entering, could have legal recourse against those who impair or cause that innocence to degenerate."

"By default, the law must presume the innocence of the soul. Now that it is legally recognized, new laws must be framed so that they protect that innocence."

Grillon emptied his glass. "People will think twice about having children, they could be liable for conspiracy to corrupt an individual … just by bringing them up wrong."

"Just by being a negative influence or a poor role model!" added Margeaux.

As the conjecture continued, Eya daydreamed of ephemeral beings descending from a higher abode, transported to their place of birth and entering a newborn host.

"Oh look, on the holo … it's about the Enlightenment!" said Margeaux excitedly.

They all turned toward an image of the Great Hall of the Center of Truth growing in clarity within the wall-size projection space of the holo-viewer.

"… has been released and we can now confirm the methodology of the scientific research."

Silence gripped the dining room.

The Orator took the podium and began his confirmation. To accompany him, a stream of visual evidence began to display.

Pictures of medical research establishments, a prone figure lying on an electrically charged platform ... scientists dressed in isolation suits.

The most trusted figure in the Free World explained in a quiet and compelling tone, "... experiments, painstakingly performed over the preceding decades, involving the use of DNA replication technology for cloning a human being, and also the quantum imaging of electric ionization boosted by stochastic resonance ..."

He described with intricate detail how the research into cloning higher life-forms, such as human beings, had for years not progressed beyond creating an "empty shell." Lower life-forms, such as sheep, pigs and even tool-wielding apes had been cloned in two ways. One, by implanting a DNA-altered embryo into a surrogate mother, and secondly, by incubating an altered egg to full maturity in an artificial gestation chamber.

But even those simple animals had to be "revived" from the gestation chamber in order to bring them to life. And although science had found a way to replicate the process of procreation, it still could not claim to have *created* life. It had just replaced an organic link in the chain with an artificial one. A viable, living egg had still been required.

Further, no sentient life-form capable of cognitive thought – or self-awareness, had been artificially cloned with success. An altered human embryo had only survived when gestation had been completed organically – within a human mother – until now.

The background history complete, the Orator raised his hand, "But that organic process didn't prove how the 'life-force' belonging to the newborn came to be in the host. Perhaps it had simply *generated* from within, an inherent form of energy – a new mind awakened within an electro-chemical host, the brain."

He then continued to describe how the critical evidence in the discovery came from a secondary branch of research using quantum imaging. Its origins lay in neural imaging techniques, and the controversial Kirlian effect, where images captured the "aura" of the departed component from a torn leaf. In a complex and high-risk experiment, a terminally-ill patient's heart was stopped using a lethal depolarization impulse from a defibrillation device.

Once the volunteer, laying on an electrically-charged platform, was confirmed as deceased, revival of the clone in an adjacent gestation chamber began.

The dinner guests watched in fascination as the Kirlian imaging showed the ghostly shade of the departed human male leave the body laying prone on the platform. Then, as a medical team anxiously attempted to resuscitate the intended host, the clone – the ethereal form slowly moved across the few feet separating the two bodies … and simultaneously entered its now reviving host.

∞

St. Querin, Germany
July 1945

The pfederställe at the villa in St. Querin were typical for housing the many horses of the Bavarian nobility. A long stone building with rows of stables interspersed by tack and feed rooms. Colonel Blackett stopped in the breezeway to admire a huge but docile black warmblood.

"He's a Percheron from Western France," General Patton pointed out. "They make excellent hunters."

Blackett stroked the wide forehead, having to brush aside the large handful of forelock to reveal the kind eyes below. Although he had a reputation in the OSS of being a stone-cold killer, animals always brought out his softer side.

His smile faded as he heard Patton add, "Heavy horses like

this one had been used to trample infantry in the Middle Ages."

As they walked along the barn the General felt compelled to share his thoughts on the information he'd gathered from Major Rhuzkoi on the morning ride.

"The Russkies still have a sizeable army of occupation in Eastern Europe. We're going to need a different strategy than the one we used to beat the Nazis."

"I agree. Though there are civilian reports we've gathered from people crossing the border from the East – that there are mass desertions from the Red Army."

"What? Going home because there aren't enough civilians left for them to rape?"

"Regardless of the reasons for the desertions," Blackett continued, "Stalin is infiltrating communists into the governments of the countries they occupy. We can expect there may be political, and even military resistance from some of those quarters."

Patton pondered for a moment, then said dismissively, "Those that have any military forces intact. If they were fighting alongside the Germans, like the Hungarians and the Romanians did, then they won't have much left to fight with."

They walked out of the stables and into the cool, late summer air. Stopping at a gate leading into the paddock, Blackett could see why the General had chosen this place as his headquarters. The meadow beyond positively glowed with lush green grass, stretching all the way to the shadowed dark of the forest.

"We'll have all of our data ready for your trip to Washington," he said with conviction.

"Good. The critical piece is the document we received from the RLA – the evidence we have of an impending attack by the Soviets. That'll silence any doubters that may have the President's ear. Then the Commander in Chief can concentrate on the influencers in Congress."

The General stood as tall and somber as a bronze statue, steel blue eyes gazing out over the rural setting as though he were storing the image for later use. Perhaps to him it was a kind of Eden, an ideal to keep him going while he endured the upcoming process of getting politicians to see his way of thinking.

"Our hope is that once they are convinced of the threat we face here ... then the continuation of strategic war production will only be a formality."

Blackett agreed, "And I'm sure with your influence in the General Staff there will be little opposition to getting priority given to your specific programs."

"There better not be. Air power isn't going to be an issue, or getting the T32s to full production, but if we don't get the new 203mm SPs we need, then the ground war will be very difficult."

Blackett nodded, but Patton sensed he wanted to hear more.

"Those 203s have a high angle of fire – so they can hit the rear side of hills."

He smirked. "I don't expect we'll see much of the Reds front on ... they'll be behind hills or hiding underground, not out in the open where we can just roll right over them."

A thoughtful silence followed, as the two men soaked up the atmosphere of the peaceful meadow and horses grazing blithely nearby, oblivious to the apocalyptic planning occurring just out of earshot.

Patton shivered, although the heat from the bright sunshine was palpable.

"As Napoleon once said ... *to extraordinary circumstances we must apply extraordinary remedies.*"

∞

Mojave City
2265 CE

The speculation after dinner had been vibrant after the

Enlightenment's follow-up demonstration. What had they actually seen? Was it a collection of photons held together by some inter-dimensional force? If part of the soul existed in another dimension, and that dimension was accessible from this one ... then there must be some transitional state.

"So we saw the patient's soul detaching from the mind of the original body, then moving to the clone – a new host ... with a completely empty mind?" asked Grillon.

"Yes – apparently the patient has the mental state of a newborn baby," Arjon responded, reading a news update from his hand-held.

"All of this is going to be too hard ..." Eya pointed out, thinking way ahead as she tended to do.

"How will people know what impact their words or actions are having on innocent children?"

"Hmmm ... we'll need a decision matrix for the human mind!" Arjon offered.

"I'm sure the Bureau of Sanity will already be working on it."

"No seriously ..." Eya giggled, and then suddenly frowned, "Oh, we can't let the BoS get a hold of this."

"That's their job," said Arjon flatly. "And yes, if there is an ideal mental state to which we should aspire –a healthy mind and contented soul – then let that also be a definition of our sanity."

"But ... they're so ... *logical!*" she protested.

Arjon laughed. Logic and judgment went hand in hand for him. One of the reasons he worked with the law was that to him, they were inseparable. Even if a verdict had in some way been influenced by emotion, or a supposed sense of justice ... you could always define it logically. Rationalize it. The heart belonged in paintings and literature, not government and law making.

"The Bureau of Sanity has held the world together. More so than the Union of Nations or *any* of the other pillars of our society!"

"You know full well that I disagree with that," Eya reminded him. "The Spire of Evolution has led the world to where it is now. Would we have attained this utopia … this *nirvana*, without guiding the human form into a flawless state?"

"Yes, I suppose there is some merit in that line of thinking," he conceded, "… with no disease or infection, and the achievement of near-perfect cellular replication, the social burdens that result from our physical degeneration no longer afflict us."

"We still don't know how long we can expect to live – over five hundred years is the latest estimate," added Grillon, looking thoughtfully into his wine glass.

Eya sighed, it was pointless to try to compare the Pillars. Deep down she might have even believed the Center of Truth had the foremost role in humanity's ascent from chaos. Their role as the administrators of both scientific verification and spiritual confirmation, two disciplines who were previously in opposition to each other, had been pivotal in keeping the other pillars in sync. She remembered playing a game with the other little girls called "Round the Stump." One girl would sit down away from the other girls, who would take turns skipping around the "pillar" girl in a relay. The pillar would slowly rise to a standing position, but have to sit down again if the skipping girl finished in time. Then another girl became the pillar, and so on, until they all got too tired to finish.

The pillar girl keeping the others in sync … I wish the world was that simple.

The voices around the table drew her attention back.

"… Without directed evolution as a framework then we're simply following natural selection," said Grillon, "which is always at the mercy of a chaotic nature – a slave that can never be free of its master."

"But where might that lead us? Should we sever our relationship with the natural environment completely? Hmm

... think of the Enlightenment – instead of clones, we could start hosting ourselves in machines, and take nature out of the equation altogether," countered Macrose, another of Arjon's colleagues.

Okay now we're getting too heavy, Eya thought, and returned to her less serious reflection. She had a moment of pure joy as she remembered one of their dinner party discussions from years ago. They had asked, "Was it that science has progressed to a height where it could now prove the spiritual mysteries of the past? Or has spirituality descended to a level where it can now be scientifically proven?"

"Neither!" they'd cried in unison. It was one of those moments when the couple did not need words to confirm mutual understanding, their champagne and caviar consensus had concluded that the two concepts, science and spirituality, had been elevated to a point where they could both see each other from their loftier vantage points.

∞

Mannheim, Germany
December 14th, 1945

A dry and bitterly cold morning greeted Elsa Huber as she opened the front door of her lodgings. She paused to put on her mittens and wrapped her woolen scarf a little tighter around her neck, then began her regular walk to the café on Duden Strasse.

US Army trucks passed by, splashing up mud from freshly thawed puddles. Elsa checked her stockings for any spots, drawing a wolf-whistle from one the drivers at the sight of a knee. She blushed, and continued on in a slight hurry.

The street ran parallel to a railway line. She spied an approaching locomotive as it came down the line toward her. Beyond the billowing column of charcoal gray smoke she could see it was another trainload of armored vehicles and artillery.

So many trains full of tanks and soldiers. I thought the war was over?

She went into the café and ordered some tea. It was much busier than it had been during the war. The nearby army depot brought in both GIs from the Occupation Forces, and Red Cross nurses. It made for a noisier atmosphere than she preferred, but at least the nurse's presence meant that the soldiers would leave her alone.

Elsa watched out the window as the last car of the train passed through a crossing. The thin dusting of snow between the tracks was whipped up into the frigid, dry air in whirling flurries. Orange and blue flitted through the snow, as sparks spat and crackled up from the rails.

A soldier approached her table and asked if the seat opposite her was taken.

"Yes ... I'd prefer to sit on my own if you don't mind."

He smiled politely, but was clearly put out. Elsa turned back to the window to avoid the soldier's forlorn gaze. She noticed a car bearing down on the railway crossing. It was a big American model, the kind she'd seen high ranking officers being driven around in. Just as it went over the rails there was a bright flash ... *lightning?*

The car halted suddenly, tires screeching. *Perhaps it was a burst of static electricity from the tracks,* she thought. Then she stood up, startled, as a three-ton truck barreled over the crossing just in front of the car, narrowly missing it.

The sounds from the near-miss had everyone in the café on their feet, so Elsa, following them, went outside. Within minutes military policemen from the depot arrived and cleared the spectators from around the car. Word quickly spread through the throng that an important US General had been in the car. Elsa didn't hear the name clearly, *General Parton was it?*

She weaved her way deeper into the huddle, fighting against

her own discomfort more than the other onlookers. She was intrigued. The bright light at the time of the near-miss. Was she the only one who saw it?

Now within earshot of the truck's driver being interviewed by one of the policemen, she heard him say, "It was weird ... I was almost blinded. Before I knew it I'd driven straight across in front of that car ... lucky we missed them."

"Sure pal. And have you been drinking?" asked the MP.

Voices from the crowd, many of them off-duty servicemen, quickly grew into a murmur of accusation.

The MP called out, "Look – the General's okay – only some bruises – everyone go back to your own business."

The driver was quickly ushered away by the Military Police and the noise began to peter out. As Elsa walked over the road to the café her mind was full of the images from the incident. She felt a shiver run down her spine, but it was not from the cold.

∞

Order is a rebellion against chaos.
Mantra of the Union of Nations

Mojave City
2265 CE

"Hesta, I want a summary of the potential damages that Sargent Harrison would have incurred due to the accident."

"Certainly, there will be a speculative factor of thirteen point nine percent."

"Fine. We'll deduct that from the fiscal outcomes."

Moments later a report materialized in front of Arjon. He glanced at the early paragraph, skipping over the more obvious consequences of a prematurely terminated career in the Signal Corps. That was followed by a summary of the Sargent's activity as he spent twelve months "laying low," and all of the limitations to employment he was subjected to, along with the economic hardship he had endured.

"Hmmm, looks like there is a solid case for compensation for our client. Please add this to the final report. You'll need to trim it a little so it fits our standard template ... but be sure to leave the most important points, then, add reference links to the finer detail."

"Please confirm the list of central items."

A holo-list popped up in front of Arjon and he read it through. The top few rows showed the plaintiff's complaint in summary. Foremost, the financial hardship and the injury to the reputation of Sargent Harrison, allegedly caused by the negligence of the Military Police.

By being responsible for the loss of one of their records, and subsequently not clearing up any indications that their soldier, Sargent Harrison, was in any way at fault in General Patton's accident, there was a case for compensation against the Military Police, and hence the US Army.

Arjon mused on the likely outcome. With the sometimes-extensive timeframes involved in genealogical cases, the legal remedy may only be intangible. A statement made which restores the reputation of the plaintiff. The defendant may no longer be alive, or exist as a legal entity to be sued.

In this case that wouldn't be a problem. Although it hadn't been called upon by the Union of Nations in a very long time, the Pentagon was still just off Washington Boulevard.

"These are fine, but change the position of the line about the accident report – a standard military document logged by the Military Police being 'misplaced.' Move it up two places. It's the critical piece of evidence."

"Understood."

"Oh, and don't forget to add a copy of the accident report as Appendix A."

This area of Genealogical Litigation was Arjon's bread and butter. A piece of evidence, a document or visual record, comes to light after hundreds of years, the existence of which would have a significant impact on a person's life. In this case, a family from Pennsylvania, the direct descendants of a soldier involved in an incident over three centuries ago had filed the complaint. The incident had involved a significant historical figure: General George S. Patton.

Sargent Harrison was the driver of the truck which had narrowly missed Patton's staff car. However, he had been blamed for the accident and had to disappear. Although Patton had received only minor injuries, rumors immediately spread that Harrison had been drinking. The fact that he had almost killed the most important General in the US Army meant that people were out for his blood, and he vanished accordingly.

Now ... in the year 2265, a critical report of the accident, lodged by the Military Police who attended the scene of the crash, had finally surfaced. The report stated that the Sargent's blood alcohol level had been zero.

"Report processing complete," Hesta said. "Would you like me to delete the matrix?"

"No, not yet ... I'm curious about the ongoing significance of this incident."

He had a sudden yearning to be back in the late 1940s. A time when so many events had occurred that shaped the world, and the centuries that followed. He daydreamed of being an invisible observer, floating above the Earth and watching as the struggling and suffering people of the time made their way through those momentous trials.

Due to the recent improvement in Hesta's virtualization performance, Arjon's work on this case was completed early, so he allowed himself to do something with his research he wouldn't normally do – he speculated.

What if the accident had been fatal?

∞

February 13th, 1946
Near Linz, Austria

The cone of light from a steamtrain's headlamp wound its way through a snow-covered valley. The plume of steam from its engine disappeared into the starless night sky, as Colonel William Blackett scanned the heavens. Snowflakes falling in heavy clusters peppered the exposed part of his face as he looked up hopefully at the gray void.

Just keep it up for another day ... or even two.

The snow whipped up around him in flurries, driven by the slipstream of the relentless train. Lowering his gaze, he strained to catch a glimpse of the lone red tail light on the guard car he knew to be almost half a mile astern. He felt assured by the obscured blackness between him and the unseen light, *zero visibility ... couldn't be better.*

He turned and went back into the dimly lit shelter of the carriage. No heating, but the air was warmed by the bodies swathed in thick brown coats and woolen balaclavas. These were the officers and senior NCOs, the enlisted men were huddled in the boxcars. He unraveled the scarf from around his face and looked up the aisle. Most of the men were asleep, but a few met his eye. It struck him that those eyes looking back at him held that quality of purpose ... a tempered edge. Something within them that ordinary soldiers didn't have. But these weren't elite troops. Many had been recruited from German POW camps after being captured on the Eastern front fighting for the Red Army. Now in the RLA, they'd been through hell ... and had willingly returned to go through it all again if they had to.

Considered traitors by their homeland, if caught, no doubt Stalin would have them sent to labor camps from which they would not return. Blackett admired them for what they had done ... and for what they were about to do.

He passed through four more similarly packed cabins until he reached the foremost carriage reserved for the senior officers. No extra comfort here. The same unfinished timber as the other unheated economy class compartments.

He took his seat next to a dozing Major Rhuzkoi and then closed his eyes.

Another two hours till we reach Enns, then unload 45 tanks in the total darkness. This is going to be fun.

At midnight the train reached a junction and pulled into a freight depot on a siding. No lights or whistles ... just the blowing hiss of pressurized steam being released into the blizzard, and the sound carried away on the blustering wind.

The nearby sleeping town of Enns had seen hundreds of similar trains pass through in the previous weeks, but not all stopped at this siding. Many continued through to Steyn, where the US Third Army was building up for "maneuvers."

The clang of wheels rolling through the switched junction roused Colonel Blackett and those around him. Major Rhuzkoi looked at his watch and pulled the shade, craning to peer through the glowing darkness.

"On time," he said. "There's something to be said for Austrian efficiency."

Colonel Blackett nodded, "Yes, almost as good as the Swiss. Hey ... Swiss watches ... Austrian cuckoo clocks – you think there's something with that and the trains being on time?"

Rhuzkoi looked puzzled.

"Eh ... because of making clocks?" he asked.

"Sure ... clocks – trains running on time ... get it?"

Blackett shrugged, still not having figured out if Russians don't like to shoot the breeze, or just don't have a sense of humor.

He dropped the levity. "We should be disembarked and get to the bivouac before daylight."

Rhuzkoi looked pleased without smiling. "General Vlasov

will be very glad to hear of this. All of the divisions in his army will be at full strength when we reach him tomorrow night."

"And if this weather holds up … H-Hour will go ahead as scheduled," added Blackett.

Two Lieutenant Colonels sitting opposite spoke no English, so listened without expression. An aide came up from a radio post at the front of the car and handed the Major a message. He studied it.

"Excellent! It is from the partisans at the bridge. They describe the road conditions from there onwards as stable."

"They won't be after we've taken our convoy through," said Blackett drily.

Several hours of urgent activity followed, with two thousand troops and twenty platoons of tanks being unloaded. The temporary depot had been specially prepared with additional cranes for handling the frequent delivery of large numbers of armor and other vehicles.

The RLA convoy left the depot well before dawn and entered another prepared site a few miles away inside a forest. They spent the following day loading up with the supplies and fuel that had awaited them there. At dusk, the column set out on the thirty-mile journey to link up with the RLA divisions already across the border in northern Austria.

The first twenty miles would be uneventful, even in a snowstorm with icy roads. Once they reached the Danube, things could get more dangerous. Secrecy was essential. It was possible communist spies had already reported their presence here, but they would be just another convoy of US armor involved in the maneuvers. Once across the river which formed the border, they would be in Soviet-occupied territory. Once there, they would need to conceal their movements … or else deal with any patrols which happened upon them. Discovery at such a precarious stage of the operation would be disastrous.

Blackett looked once again up into the sheltering blizzard.

Was the snowfall relenting?

∞

Mojave City
2265 CE

Arjon hadn't felt so intrigued, so *inspired,* since his days at the university. He'd been poring over the possibilities generated by the probability core of the matrix for hours. General George S. Patton had been the most influential military leader of the twentieth century, and as Arjon watched the simulations play out, he searched his own memory of that period of history. *Yes ... there were suggestions that he had somehow influenced the political climate after the Second World War ... something about the fortuitous build-up of his army's military strength ... when one would have expected widespread disarmament.*

"Hesta, run a more detailed simulation – one that demonstrates the effects on global political and military decision making during the period following the General's accident – with a single change in parameterization ..."

"I will not have sufficient processing power to perform that enquiry in isolation. It will require my accessing the neural resources of the regional network. Confidentiality may be compromised."

"No matter, its pure speculation and the incidental content of the case does not have to be included. Proceed."

The regional neural network, or meganet, had eventuated over a century ago, from a need for massive processing power for an unfunded research project. By pooling the resources of millions of personal computers and other communication devices connected over the primitive internet, the project distributed packets of data to be processed by each node. The concept grew, until now there were billions of nodes linked to form the most powerful neural processor on the planet. In a world with no poverty or crime, there were no security concerns, so the meganet was accessible to anyone.

"Reconstructing matrix with the new probability algorithm. Awaiting parameter input ..."

Arjon worded his changes carefully, "General George S. Patton died as a result of injuries received in the car accident on December 14th 1945."

"Parameter accepted. Matrix completion estimated in thirty-two hours."

∞

February 14th, 1946
Near Enns, Austria

A long line of Sherman tanks, mobile artillery and Studebaker trucks carrying troops and supplies moved steadily into the night. Blackett and Rhuzkoi rode near the lead in an M3A1 scout car.

"Did the partisans mention the condition of the bridge?" the OSS Colonel asked.

"*Nyet*, but I am sure it will be serviceable. All other convoys have crossed without incident."

"Sure ... but that's a lot of armor already putting their weight onto it ... and some of that was your RLA's Russian built stuff. You know – heavier and clunkier than these Shermans," said Blackett giving the Major an elbow in the ribs.

Rhuzkoi might have understood the Colonel's attempt at a jibe, but still no smile lifted his stern Ukrainian jawline.

After a thoughtful moment he replied gravely, "Colonel ... you are implying that the engineering of our glorious T-34 is somehow ... crude?"

Blackett wasn't sure if he'd offended his ally. He was about to apologize when Rhuzkoi burst out laughing.

"Ha! Your face is like little boy! The *smyekh* ... how you say – the laugh, is on you! *Da!*"

Blackett smirked. *So he has a sense of humor after all.*

"Da Valentin ... the *joke* – the joke is on me."

The clean white corridor of the frozen Danube loomed ahead from out of the comforting drift of snowflakes.

Without stopping, the column continued from the road's end and out onto the river of ice.

Blackett braced himself as if the scout car could break through the crust any second, plunging them into the subzero water below, and certain death.

He looked down from the passenger side door and spied a row of thin black stakes being used as a guideline by the driver. Just a few feet beyond, he could make out the cracked and jagged surface of the river, caused by shifting ice floes moving slowly beneath a deceptive blanket of white.

"Wait a sec ... why aren't we ..."

"Breaking through? Ha! Your face again!" laughed the Russian.

"It's an underwater bridge," he said. "One of several built by the Red Army in 1945 when they attacked through here on their way to Vienna."

Blackett had heard of these "bridges." A roadway of dirt and gravel bulldozed to a level just below the waterline so they weren't visible from the air, and with buried pipes to allow the water to continue flowing beneath.

"Handy ... it's no wonder the previous RLA crossings haven't been discovered. Don't the Bolsheviks know about it?"

"*Nyet* ... it was forgotten. We had to ... how do you say ... *renyovate* it? In this weather it is easily concealed. The crushed ice from the tank tracks just refreezes and is then covered by more snow."

The convoy of over two hundred vehicles took an hour to traverse the bridge. When the last vehicle exited, a group of partisans rushed out and began to gather the markers. They were accompanied by horse and cart, into which the stakes were hastily thrown.

Previous crossings had required a more rigorous cleanup.

In clearer weather, the partisans made several passes over the frozen ruts made by the tanks, raking in fresh snow from the sides to cover the fresh tracks.

Safely across the Danube, the column was now in hostile territory.

∞

Mojave City
2265 CE

"Hesta, it's been over thirty-six hours, why so long?" asked Arjon.

"The extenuating circumstances are such that most, if not all, of recent human history is being rewritten."

"From one man's actions? That's *very* interesting."

He thought of a documentary he'd seen where the meganet had been used to produce a more far-reaching example of alternative events than that which Hesta was working on.

In that case, Alexander the Great chose not to attack the Persian Empire, but instead stayed and consolidated Greece's influence in the Mediterranean. The effects had been disastrous for subsequent world events. Democracy, and many other positive facets of Greco-Roman culture, had failed to propagate throughout the species.

The documentary proposed that a world dominated by the more reactionary Eastern philosophies, such as Confucianism, or far worse – Bushido, would have eventuated.

Arjon shuddered at the thought of the militaristic Samurai shaping human history. *Shoguns and stunted feet ... geez – thank you Alexander.*

∞

February 14th, 1946
Near Enns, Austria

As the column left the Danube behind, the slotted headlights on all vehicles were turned off. The drivers would have to complete the remainder of the journey using only the limited night-vision given by the faint glow of the surrounding snow. Fortunately, they only had twenty miles to go before reaching their destination in the partisan-controlled mountains.

At the rear of the convoy several trucks and an M26 tank recovery vehicle comprised the ordnance unit. Trained by the US Army in the preceding months, it was their task to look after any breakdowns. Before crossing the Danube, these had simply been abandoned on the roadside in friendly country. Now they had to either be got going again, or else towed away from the road and into the trees, and then covered with camouflaged netting to reduce the chance of discovery.

Inside the M3A1, Blackett was elated. He reveled in this kind of underground operations – of being behind enemy lines, where a small team can cause a disproportionate amount of mayhem.

Rather than trying to get any sleep, he watched out the window and soaked up the darkness, so essential to covering their activity. He was ever mindful of all the contingencies which could ruin their progress – breakdowns, accidents, the worsening weather … patrols.

With these in mind he speculated to Rhuzkoi. "Well, at least if this scout car breaks down we won't need to hide it – we sold thousands of them to the Red Army."

"*Da* … although we never had any in my old unit. We saw many of your US tanks in other divisions, and of course the Studebakers."

Blackett continued to run the possibilities over in his mind, searching for anything they might have missed. The earlier columns had also been comprised of the trucks and tanks sold to the Reds under Lend Lease. Would that arouse suspicion if they were spotted? Would the locals even know the difference between theirs and the Russian built vehicles? There had been so little information coming from Eastern Europe since the war's end – a world growing steadily colder and darker as the Kremlin sought to distance itself from its cooperation with the Allies.

An intersection came out of gloom without warning. Still at full speed, they followed the lead armored car through the junction. In the cab, heads snapped to the left in unison as down a side road in the distance, a pair of headlights glimmered.

"Pull over!" cried Blackett.

The car slowed and stopped on the edge of the road to the right. Blackett waved the following vehicles past.

"Find room to turn around … over there!" he said, pointing to a gap in the trees.

They did a U-turn on the shoulder then sped back toward the intersection, as the column of blacked-out vehicles continued on.

Rhuzkoi pulled his balaclava up over his face so that only his eyes were visible.

In a muffled voice, he called to Blackett, "I will take the .50 caliber."

He clambered back over his seat and into the rear compartment, then stood up behind the machine gun.

Blackett checked his Colt .45, then reached over and grabbed a Thompson sub-machine gun. They turned to the left, and as they were driving without lights would not be seen by any oncoming traffic. Blackett signaled the driver to slow down and bear off the road slightly, as against the whitish backdrop, they would be spotted sooner.

The sound of tree branches whipping the side of the car gave the driver an indication that he was over far enough. The oncoming headlights increased in brightness.

Blackett thought for a moment that perhaps it might be a civilian, a farmer in his truck on the way back from the market in Bratislava.

Too bad.

The gravity of what was at stake pushed all other thoughts from his mind. Before the beam of the approaching lights hit them, he yelled, "Fire!"

Rhuzkoi opened up and the cannon-like sound of the heaviest machine gun of the war exploded into life.

Every fifth round a tracer, the Major soon found his target. Sparks and flame spattered out from the now visible patrol vehicle.

A wildly conflicting barrage of thoughts entered Blackett's mind. *Goddam that's ironic ... that's another M3A1.*

It was an earlier version of the one they were in. It seemed to wobble, almost floating above the snow-covered surface of the road ... then it swiveled on its axis and spun into the trees.

The .50 cal ceased fire abruptly and the sound of the engine returned.

The intervening seconds before they reached the wreck seemed to last for minutes. Had anyone heard the gunfire? Would there be survivors ready to open fire on them?

What were they going to do if one of them had escaped into the woods to raise the alarm? They stopped and Blackett leapt out, Thompson at the ready. He rushed up to the cab and let loose – emptying half of the clip in a wide spray from front to back of the scout car's cabin.

In the half-lit glow of the burning engine, he could only see the dim shapes of the three bodies inside jerking crazily from the bullet impacts. No survivors.

Rhuzkoi joined him and inspected the vehicle. He took some satisfaction at the sight of the shattered windscreen. Only a few rounds from the .50 cal. would have been needed to obliterate it and instantly kill the occupants.

"Let's go," said Blackett, "we'll catch up with the tail-end of the convoy and get the M26 to come back here to tow the wreck into the trees."

"*Da* ... but they'll be missed by morning. We must also radio the partisans to prepare an ambush here to cover our tracks."

"Gotcha ... that's a better idea – we'll leave it here then."

They left and soon caught the column. Rhuzkoi reluctantly broke radio silence to send a message to the partisans at the bridge. It was a game of ever-increasing risks.

The remaining cards fell in their favor, and they arrived at Königswiesen before midnight. The hamlet was ideal for this purpose, lying in a valley and flanked by heavily wooded mountains on either side. RLA troops directed them to prepared sites under thick camouflage netting in the forest lining the valley's edge.

Around them, barely visible among the trees, were the outlines of more RLA armor, including many Russian tanks. These had been recovered from the defeated German army, who in turn, had captured them from the Red Army during the preceding years of conflict.

Blackett and Rhuzkoi, along with several senior officers from the column, were led up a steep trail to a hunting lodge. It was invisible in the snow-covered darkness, until they were only a few feet away from the slips of light peeking out from behind blackout curtains.

Inside, a blazing fireplace greeted them, and RLA officers hurried about busily. A tall, bespectacled General noticed them and left a group hovering above a map table. He stepped over and embraced Major Rhuzkoi warmly.

"Comrade General," said Rhuzkoi, "this is Colonel William Blackett of the United States Office of Strategic Services."

Blackett took an offered hand, and said, "It's an honor to finally meet you General Vlasov."

"It is a mutual pleasure Colonel. We have much to thank your OSS for."

"Well General, if you are referring to your recent escape from captivity while in transit to Moscow, I'm sure all of the credit belongs to your anti-Bolshevik friends."

Vlasov chuckled appreciatively. The tall Russian had an imposing presence – the aura of a man with a purpose.

As though every minute counted, the General motioned the small group of arrivals to a circle of heavy leather chairs around the fireplace.

After a quick debrief of their expedition, and the encounter with the Red Army patrol vehicle, Blackett took the General aside and asked him about something that had been piquing his interest.

"I have a question General, please let me know if it's inappropriate, but it's about the document we passed on to General Patton. He took it with him to Washington, and it appears to have been highly effective in influencing our government's policy."

Vlasov indicated approval, also giving a quizzical look to his liaison officer. Rhuzkoi shrugged his shoulders, unknowingly.

"We don't doubt the document's authenticity ... it's just I was hoping to provide a more detailed explanation of how it was acquired."

Blackett paused, choosing his words very carefully. "You see, General Patton is an officer of the highest honor ..." another pause, both Vlasov and the Major were listening attentively. "And we're sure you would wish to maintain that honor in all of your dealings with the General."

The Russians showed no reaction, but Blackett read their body language as being positive. Chests prominent, chins outstanding ... there was no subterfuge here, they weren't hiding anything, Blackett could tell that these too, were men of honor.

"Colonel, I would explain to you with pride how we obtained the letter ..." said Vlasov, "but I cannot."

Blackett's eyebrows raised in surprise. "If it will breach confidentiality I can assure you ..."

"Colonel, we will provide you with full disclosure ... once the operation is completed," said Vlasov.

"At this stage, lives would still be at risk – important lives. You must continue to trust in the validity of the letter, and that our intentions are also ... honorable."

With that, the conference was over. General Vlasov and the officers of his command returned to the large map table, and their task of preparing for the following day ... they were off to start a war.

∞

Feb 18th, 1946
Steyr, Austria

The blare of klaxons through the trees sent a flock of sparrows fleeing from their overnight roost. The sirens heralded the arrival of the 3rd Army commander to the villa which was serving as a temporary 10th Armored Division headquarters.

His Dodge half-ton command car was followed by several limousines. On their bonnets fluttered the flags of their respective nations. The British and French military governors to Austria were here as observers. The entourage spilled out of their vehicles and exchanged greetings. They were here to see the latest additions to their US ally's arsenal – the T30 heavy tank, aptly known as the Mammoth.

One of the 64-ton giants stood with a light coating of frost in the villa's outer courtyard, near a statue of a mounted Duke Leopold VI. Its massive turret had a squarish protrusion on either side which housed the latest radar range-finding technology.

The early morning sun struggled to break through the clouds, and light snow began to fall as General Patton addressed his guests.

"Gentlemen, this tank represents one of the updates to our

armored warfare doctrine."

He slowly paced around to the front of the tank, where the long-barreled 155mm gun rested in its travel sling.

"A shift from the mobility of lightly armored medium tanks, such as the Sherman, to a thickly-armored vehicle with overwhelming firepower."

The Mammoth stood like a monument to destruction. Its metallic hull resonated an aura of indestructibility, and seemed to amplify the General's words.

"I won't' bore you gentlemen with the tactical detail … but basically this type of tank will be deployed to our GHQ tank battalions, and along with armored infantry and engineers, form the spearhead of an attack."

Lieutenant General Béthouart took off his Legionnaire hat and dusted off a few errant snowflakes.

"Mon General, does this mean that your stalwart Sherman tank is now obsolete?"

"I'm afraid so … the lessons learned while beating the Germans have manifested themselves in this weapon platform."

A question from General McCreery was a little more difficult to answer, "I'm curious about how the development and mass production of such a weapon came about?" The British commander groomed his moustache thoughtfully, "After all, the war is over, and the Russians don't appear to be spoiling for a fight."

Patton laughed, "My dear General, if I asked you what the politicians in Whitehall were thinking … could you give me a straight answer?"

The British General touched the peak of his cap, acknowledging that he would get no clearer explanation than the one he'd received.

"So, Mon General … what will be following this … *spearhead*?"

Patton's voice magnified with pride as he tapped the plate armor of the T30 with his crop.

"That we will see in a later demonstration. Our armored divisions are also being equipped with the fastest and most powerful medium tanks ever produced."

He scanned the early morning sky. As if on cue, the air suddenly erupted with the roar of a flight of P57 Thunderbolt fighter bombers.

It seemed to be a signal for the day's maneuvers to start. The fading thunder from the sky was joined by a rolling boom from nearby artillery.

The crew of the Mammoth mounted up and the 700hp Continental engine roared to life.

General McCreery and the others moved aside as the icy ground shuddered and cracked beneath the tank's extra wide tracks.

"Over 2 feet wide!" shouted Patton above the roar, "... so they'll go right over the mud!"

∞

Mojave City
2265 CE

"Simulation complete."

"Thank you, Hesta," said Arjon. "I'd now like you to produce an enhanced version containing CGI re-enactments of the key turning points in history. Can that be completed by this evening?"

"Affirmative."

"Good! I'll see if Eya wants to stay in for a movie night."

"The presentation will be scheduled to follow your evening meal."

"Nothing too filling. I want to leave room for popcorn."

∞

Feb 18ᵗʰ, 1946
Steyr, Austria

The T30 Mammoth rolled over a hill and out of sight as a flight of fighter bombers flew overhead. The exercise was now in full swing.

The group of high-ranking officers and dignitaries sat on a viewing platform overlooking a snow-covered plain bordered by evergreen forest. The forest's edge concealed a line of concrete bunkers and anti-tank emplacements – the entrenched enemy. US infantry occupied this line, acting in the defensive role of Red Force. Moving irrevocably toward them, Blue Force, a brigade of Mammoth's together with their ground support troops.

Simulating a real attack, the smoke rounds from the heavy tanks scored hit after hit from long range … well before they would have been under fire from the smaller caliber anti-tank fire. Gun emplacements withered under the barrage, and bunkers were systematically reduced by Blue Force's cooperating units of armor and engineers.

The visitors in the stands watched and talked excitedly, clearly impressed by what they were seeing. In the front row, however, sitting next to Patton, General McCreery shifted uneasily.

The ominous display prompted him to voice a concern. "General Patton, I wonder if a tank this powerful may provoke alarm, even an overreaction, from the Soviets …"

"My government doesn't think so General. In fact, they're now more concerned with the sorry fate of Eastern European countries resulting from communist muscle-flexing … and the Soviet's recalcitrance at the negotiations over the United Nations."

"It's widely known you have significant influence in Washington General. Can you elaborate on how your government's foreign policy is shaping this clearly overwhelming show of force?"

Another squadron of fighter bombers flew overhead with a deafening roar.

McCreery couldn't make out what Patton said, except for "… 'uck up those goddammed Bolsheviks …"

As the 3rd Army exercise continued deeper into the forest, General Patton stood up in the front row, facing the gathering he was about to address, when an aide came running up from a nearby communications post.

"General!" shouted the aide, rushing onto the platform.

Patton looked at him with some surprise at the interruption, but waited for an explanation.

"Sir! It's the Russians!" said the aide both breathlessly and loudly enough for everyone to hear, "They've just crossed the border and are attacking towards Linz!"

The crowd, shocked at the news, began jumping to their feet. Then, as though they were suddenly struck by the magnitude of it, in unison they turned toward General Patton, standing before them like a rock.

The American General called to them in an unnaturally calm voice. "By God … those bastards don't know what they're in for."

∞

Mojave City
2265 CE

"Popcorn?" asked Arjon as he settled down next to Eya.

She ducked her hand into the bowl and a few spilled into his lap. Picking those up while he prepped the playback, he asked her, "How was your afternoon in the studio?"

"Oh alright, I didn't get much done … still a little drained. I spent some time searching through archives for some inspiration."

"Wow ... that sounds tedious for you ... find anything?"

"Not for my work. But I found a centuries-old proverb ... I thought it was appropriate for the new Enlightenment."

"Oh really?"

"Yes ..., '*To be alone and without love ... is a wasted body. To not be alone, without love ... is a wasted soul.*'"

Arjon smiled. "Wonderful, and yes, so appropriate."

As he finished setting up Hesta's simulation, he mused, "There are still those who struggle to live the Ideal ... who fall by the wayside, or into decadence, and have to depend on the Pillars for guidance."

Eya sighed, "Lost souls ... well, perhaps being more enlightened will help them to find a more meaningful purpose."

"Alright, here we go ..." Arjon said.

"What? No BlindFold?" asked Eya.

"I thought we should do without the intensity of VR. This could be very disturbing."

"Okay then," Eya agreed, gripping Arjon's hand. "I'm ready."

At first the images are in black and white, inducing the viewer to interact with the era more readily. The first few scenes flow by, accompanied by a commentary from a simulated Humphrey Bogart voice-over.

Images of world leaders of the time, Roosevelt, Hitler, Stalin and Churchill, are interspersed with enhanced archival footage of significant events.

The stage is set. Now the simulations begin.

A wall is built in Berlin, Chinese communists invade a peaceful Tibet. Jewish children, survivors from the Holocaust, hunger-strike aboard a rusty freighter in the Mediterranean so they can be allowed to enter Palestine.

Eya cries in horror, "Oh my! What *was* that?"

"We can go back in more detail later ... I did say this may be distressing."

The chaos continues.

Chinese communists implement collectivism which leads to a famine causing the death by starvation of tens of millions of their people. A primitive spherical satellite orbits the Earth, tanks crush their own citizens in a city square, millions are massacred in Rwanda, the flagship of an environmental group is bombed in a New Zealand harbor by French Special Forces.

The two gentle utopians watch in horror as the Earth unravels from the clean, tranquil, prosperous world they know ... into an alternative of dysfunctional insanity.

Eya snuggles closer and looks up at Arjon, "Makes you appreciate what we have doesn't it?"

He can't speak. Transfixed by sorrow and compassion for the human race, he can't believe such a change could be attributed to the events surrounding just one man.

Eya squeezes his hand, "Whose life was it you said had made all of the difference?"

Arjon, wiped a tear from his eyes, "A General ..." and then the enormous irony hit home.

"Man ... what a paradox."

"So, what did he do that was important enough to change the world?"

"Not just him ... it was the butterfly effect ... everything that flowed on from the events in the late 1940s ... until today – because he survived a car accident."

Arjon sighed, exhausted. They were both emotionally drained. Although they were used to experiencing virtual reality using the BlindFold, the simulation had been more intense ... it had burned deeper ... because they could both sense the truth when they were seeing it.

"Can you take any more of this, or do you need to see something lighter?"

"Lighter, yes ... an episode of Asteroid Renovations ... and something nice!"

"Nice and light ... coming up."

Arjon went to the bower's replenishment bar. Hesta had already prepared Eya's favorite, Cocoa soufflé with vanilla-bean cream. Arjon asked the AI to make him the same.

"As its not to your usual taste I wasn't sure if that's what you wanted ... your serotonin levels are outside of your usual profile ... but diagnosis indicates that ingestion of tryptophan will be beneficial to your biorhythm – hence the egg whites in the soufflé."

"As long as it's unsweetened it'll be fine. Thank you Hesta."

He returned to the recreation space to find Eya already in a better mood. She accepted the dessert gratefully.

"I'd be interested to know more about your General," she said, "... but without any simulations. Just some history – documentary style."

"I'll have Hesta look it up. My research from the case was specific to the time of the accident. I believe there was mention of his influence in Washington. Then Arjon thought for a moment, and added, "... and of course he was involved in the wars in the twentieth century ... I remember that from my elementary history."

"Good ... bring it up at the next dinner party ... I'm sure Grillon and Margeaux will be enthralled!"

∞

... and the orbs
Of his fierce chariot rolled, as with the sound
Of torrent floods, or of a numerous host.
Paradise Lost
John Milton

Feb 18th, 1946
Jihlava, Czechoslovakia

A postcard from winter – a lonely road ringed by square miles of white wedding-cake icing, is watched over by frosted pine trees. The muffled echo of an axe cutting through brittle wood splits the early morning silence.

Several blows, then a loud crack follows the final swing. The snap of elastic cables precedes the hollow thump of tall timber dropping into a snow bank.

A grin of missing teeth flash from beneath a thick black beard at the sight of the fallen telegraph pole. The peasant shoulders his axe and starts retracing his footprints back to the tree-line. He knows at the same time on a dozen other roads in southern Czechoslovakia, his partisan brothers are also severing the telegraph lines.

The main communications are now cut between Prague and several key towns, including Brno, Jihlava and Tábor. A zone from south-east to south-west of the capital is now enclosed in unseen isolation.

Efreiter Ilya Grigorovich squints against the reflected glare from the morning sun on the snow. A Defender of Leningrad, his survival of the intervening years on the Eastern Front only came about through the good fortune of being assigned to the duties of Ambulance driver.

With the end of the war came a fall in demand for those services. Deciding to stay in the Red Army for the regular pay, he was at this moment regretting that decision, as he did almost every day. He could be sitting beside a fire in the Urals instead of standing atop a guard tower outside this little town in Czechoslovakia.

Tramping his feet on the steel mesh floor of the forty-foot high platform to keep warm, he chuckles at the previous night's debauchery. Re-living his exploits in the town with his comrades always gives him comfort on his lonely vigils. There had to be some compensation for being sent to this frozen outpost, and after all, Josef Stalin himself had condoned the widespread rape of the conquered womenfolk.

That was not surprising, as he'd heard stories of Stalin's Chief of NKVD, Lavrentiy Beria, being chauffeur-driven through the streets around the Kremlin so he could select women to take back to his apartment for "special" treatment.

Ah, such a time to be a proud member of the victorious Soviet military.

The sky is clear, but the sun is still too low on the horizon to provide any radiant heat. He lifts his field glasses and does a routine scan along the road stretching into the distance.

Is that a vehicle approaching?

Sometimes a large deer would wander out of the trees, and in the glimmering haze resemble a car. He watches as the dark shape wavers in the dazzling glare from the snow.

It seems to be growing, and getting ... longer.

His brain, still slightly addled from last night's alcohol saturation, tells him it might be a serpent, a Zilant, winding its way toward him. He puts down his glasses and moves to the telephone.

Dead.

He turns to look down the road again, "*Klyaat*! There are hundreds of them!"

A sound begins to rise up, drowning out the bleakness of his solitude. It is a sound he hasn't heard for many months ... since the battle for Vienna.

Artillery!

The rushing crescendo of a speeding train screams in his ears. His last thoughts are not of his nightly drunken plundering, but of the terror of shelling, of cowering in trenches, shin-deep in blood, urine, shit and mud.

The freight train arrives as the guard tower disintegrates amidst multiple explosions. A storm of metal beams and railings rains out in every direction. The surrounding white accepts the wreckage, and the shattered remains of Ilya, into its cold, welcoming blanket.

General Vlasov stands watching from the rear of his armored combat car. Around him, a cluster of self-propelled artillery barks and belches flame and smoke.

He feels elation. He sees the death of those soldiers ahead as the beginning of a great liberation.

First, free the Czechoslovakians, then ultimately, his own countrymen.

The booming retort of the 203mm guns rings painfully in his ears again and again. He feels no discomfort, however, only the oncoming realization of years of hope. An end to the desperate struggle to end the tyranny strangling his homeland.

He looks at his watch. Ten past nine. He could expect a progress report from his "other" army shortly. His other army, the 2nd Armored Division under the command of Major General Meandrov, whose men were wearing the same uniform as the Red Army soldiers ahead of him, should just now have crossed into Allied occupied Austria and be moving on Linz.

An opening act full of deception. He smiled at the parodox. He and the men of his RLA were playing the roles of both the villians who were starting a war, and the heroes who would finish it.

∞

Feb 18th, 1946
Linz, Austria

"Fighters!"

Plumes of snow and dirt spat up from the ground, as deadly rivulets of lead raced across the road.

"Into the trees!" screamed an officer.

White-camouflaged vehicles swerved to avoid each other as they left the congested road and sought the cover of the forest. A tank exploded, its turret hatch flew off, propelled into the air by a jet of flame.

Volleys of 130mm HVAP rockets launched from the underwing racks of P47 Thunderbolts streaked into the convoy. RLA tanks, trucks and scout cars were destroyed, and pillars of fire and black smoke erupted along the miles of road filled by the dispersing column.

From the relative safety of the trees, Major Rhuzkoi watched as the American fighter-bombers flashed past overhead. The thumping blast of anti-aircraft fire from a flak half-track followed them as they disappeared over the tree-tops.

"Too bad we have no air-force," he said with futility.

"Oh, come now Valentin," replied Colonel Blackett standing beside him. "You know they wouldn't last two minutes in these skies."

He scanned the airspace above the road to the west. Clouds were merging into a more general gray-white gloom. *Good.*

"Maybe more snow on the way ... that'll keep the bombers grounded."

"Mount up!" the Major shouted.

The column of RLA 2nd Armored Division armor resumed its march on Linz.

Minutes later, they passed through a small town on the outskirts of Linz, the streets still lined with rubble from the Red Army's spring offensive of 1945. The destruction of much of the town during the initial assault had been a violent precursor to what had followed. The Soviet soldiers had been particularly vengeful in this region – Linz was where Adolf Hitler had grown up.

Shocked civilians, their memories of the weeks of pillage and rape still vivid, retreated indoors at the sight of the new invaders. They all knew the difference between the white-circled star of the occupying US Army, and the red one painted on these vehicles.

Beyond the town, the ground opened out into a sparsely treed flat, leading up to a river. Miles ahead, the darker line of thick forest led south along the tributary of the Danube.

Blackett knew that any bridges would still be intact. That was part of the plan.

"We'll hold up here," he said to Rhuzkoi. "Have your men setup defensive positions facing to the south."

It was a poor move tactically, but they knew that. The token forces to their west would be holding the bridges, crossroads and other key points around Linz. This RLA column, and another one following the line of approach along the Danube, could easily sweep past them and take the city. That wasn't going to happen.

Blackett dismounted from the command car, and Rhuzkoi followed him. They walked a short distance toward a gentle slope. Topping the rise, they could see for several miles in the milky light of the early afternoon.

"Now we wait," said Blackett.

The major took a deep swig from a hip flask. The potato spirit, distilled by his troops in the mountains they had left during the night, was warming to the throat, bracing him against the chill air.

He offered the flask to his friend.

"But not for long," the Russian said gravely.

Raising his field glasses to the south, he gasped as an awe-inspiring sight came into focus.

Dozens of tanks followed by more than a hundred armored troop carriers approached in line-abreast formation.

Blackett passed the flask back to Rhuzkoi. "Shit we're gonna be in for it …"

The colonel lifted his glasses. He could make out the shapes of the new T32s, nicknamed the Grizzly, and a few of the slower moving heavies from the 10th Armored Division.

Blackett dropped his field glasses and looked around at their own forces. The armor comprising the RLA column, mostly older Russian KV1s, would be no match for what they would be facing.

The American troops to their west around Linz were about to see a show.

"Prepare to fire!" shouted an officer to one side.

Rhuzkoi drank again. "To tomorrow!" he toasted. "May we all live to see it!"

Blackett smiled grimly. *Amen to that ... we've got to make this look good.*

∞

RLA Czechoslovakian Offensive, Feb 1946

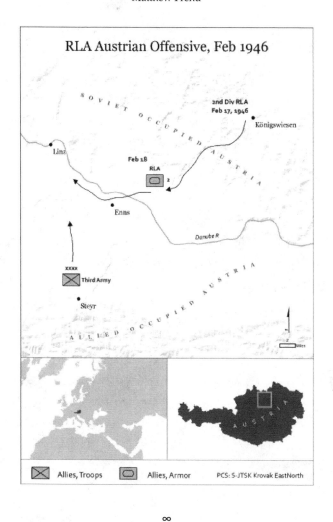

RLA Austrian Offensive, Feb 1946

∞

Prague, Russian occupied Czechoslovakia.
Feb 19th, 1946

General Ivan Fedyuninsky, Commander of the 2nd Ukrainian
Front, sipped calmly from his teacup. The aroma of Lapsang
Souchong tended to help him retain his focus.

"What is their strength?" he asked the officers seated at the
conference table around him.

"It is unknown at this stage General," answered one of his division commanders.

"We believe it must be the 3rd Army ... although reports suggest there are units of ... uncertain nationality," added another.

"Uncertain!" Fedyuninsky snapped, shedding his calm demeanor.

The officers flinched as one at the outburst. No one dared speak while the General regained his composure.

"Well ... find out. Fast!"

Notes were scribbled and passed to runners. Several left at an urgent pace for the communications department of the headquarters.

Fedyuninsky turned to a colonel from the NKVD.

"We need to inform General Secretary Stalin of the identity of the attackers ... as soon as possible."

The NKVD Colonel nodded affirmatively.

"In the meantime," the General continued, "mobilize all Divisions in the southern sector *immediately* to support those already engaged."

He glared around the table. "Bring me an updated plan to defend the approaches to Prague ..." he glanced at his watch, "... in time for a conference in four hours from now."

An officer marched into the hall carrying a signal.

"Comrade General," he said as he saluted and passed the paper to Fedyuninsky.

The 2nd Ukrainian Front Commander took another sip of tea as he read the message, then, looked searchingly around the table once again. It was as though he were looking for a victim, someone to return his glare with a shameful expression on their face and so expose their guilt.

He glanced at the note again, this time with a look of incredulity.

"Gentlemen ... this signal is from Moscow. Our government

is demanding an explanation. The Kremlin has been informed by the International News services ..." he looked despondently at his empty teacup. "It seems Lower Austria has been invaded, and that *we* have started a war."

∞

Arjon sighed heavily, expending a suppressed curse beneath his breath.

"Hesta, please stop, I can't live through any more."

The BlindFold released its light pressure from his temple and went into standby.

He closed his eyes and re-ran the previous hour of Earth's history in his mind. The events had unfolded as though the world were in the grip of a nightmare from which it could not awaken. When he compared that alternative to his own utopia, it was unnerving how easily those changes would have come about.

The Union of Nations had never really been formed. Instead, the recalcitrant communists of the Soviet Bloc had undermined the efforts to implement a truly global instrument of peace. The power of veto they attained over the Security Council meant that the UN merely became another platform for voicing the differences between conflicting ideologies.

Other critical events had revealed themselves in Arjon's memory. He could see how they would have prevented his own world coming into existence. No prosperous, enlightened decades of progress and peace through the late twentieth century, instead, the mistrust, fear, and violence had prevailed.

I need to know more ... to understand what this all means ... for us now.

"Hesta," he sighed with resignation, "I must continue ... please prepare the next instalment."

∞

Near Slavonice, Czechoslovakia
Feb 24th, 1946

Warm, acrid smoke had replaced the chill, clean air.

General Andrey Vlasov remembered the last time the clean fragrance of the forest had filled his nostrils. That had been two days ago. Now the forest was a sea of smoldering gray. The ground was bare except for snow hugging the trunks of trees, and the pockets of slick ice spread around between them, melting slowly under the heat of the fires.

They'd been retreating steadily for the past thirty-six hours. He felt no ignominy … it was part of the plan. The surprise attack on Jihlava on Day One had been followed by a twenty-mile advance toward Prague. Then the Red Army's counter offensive had begun.

Not just a small scale, reflex, counter attack – they'd been well prepared.

Sixty thousand brave men … now we are only ten thousand.

Vlasov crushed his cigarette out under his boot. He'd taken them up again during the battle after a year-long abstinence. The Russian tobacco canceled out some of the taste of the pine-smoke from the fires, but not all of it. He'd give them up when this was all over. If you had the will power to do it once, you could do it again.

A shrill whistle split the relative calm. He hit the deck, following the cigarette butt as another artillery round landed nearby. A rain of hard, frozen dirt and ice crystals showered over him. A pre-dawn barrage before another attack.

He picked himself up. As he dusted himself off, he looked over to where the shell had landed. An empty, blackened crater would have marked a clean miss, but around it were shreds of dark green cloth and streaks of bloody gore. Another RLA soldier who would not be returning home … either as a liberating freedom fighter, or in chains as a captured traitor.

A bulky, overcoated figure came rushing out of a sand-bagged command post, and began clambering up the steep slope toward him. He was bent over to help avoid the flying shrapnel and shell splinters.

"They're coming," the officer shouted. It was Vlasov's 2IC, Major General Bunyachenko. He was so exhausted by the time he reached the top of the hill, that the General couldn't tell whether he was about to laugh hysterically or begin to cry.

"Who's coming Sergei?" he urged after waiting for him to catch his breath.

"Contact … whuh, huh …, we made contact, with 3rd Army!"

For a moment, the smoke and death around him faded from Vlasov's mind, *at last!*

"When!" the General shouted, trying to be heard over the incessant barrage.

He repeated, "When will they get here?"

"Tomorrow! They're still twenty miles away, but have broken through … they've taken Brno!"

The two went downhill and into the heavily camouflaged command post.

Maps, topped by little wooded arrows and covered by dust caused by the shelling, lay scattered over a long timber table. Bunyachenko picked one up, blew off the dust and straightened it out before them. He pointed to their current position. They had fallen back to prepared defenses in the heavily forested region leading out of the valley from Königswiesen. A thirty-mile front stretching from Slavonice to Znojmo.

"We are here …" and he traced a line to the east, "… the Allied forward units are here … approaching from south of Brno."

"The Red Army's flank has been exposed, and has now been breached by the 3rd Army divisions attacking along this line … from Bratislava, through Brno … and now toward Prague."

Vlasov slapped the Major General on the back. "It is working!" he exclaimed.

"All of the months of planning ... of scheming for big surprises in the middle of the night!"

An earthquake-like shuddering sent pencils and wooden arrows dancing off the table. The muffled roar of the nearby explosion reminded them of their immediate situation.

The two men looked at each other. Vlasov's finger pointed to the map, "We'll have to withdraw further into these hills."

He drew a line from Slavonice back toward their starting point almost a week ago, "Our line will swing back towards Königswiesen here ... and pivot from our eastern flank ... here, at Znojmo."

He looked up from the map. Resolution showed on his face, as though he were willing the strategy he'd just proposed on paper, to come to fruition in the world of flame and smoke outside the bunker.

"The Bolsheviks won't follow us for fear of what would come up behind them if they did."

"*Da, da* ..." agreed Bunyachenko. "We would draw them in to the hills and extend their supply lines."

"Which would be further exposed to air attacks," added Vlasov.

Bunyachenko thought for a moment then remembered information he had omitted in the excitement of the news of their relief, "We have also been given us news of the Allied advance to the west ..."

The major General pulled out another map from beneath the others.

"From Linz, they have attacked north to Tabor, and are now swinging east below Prague."

Vlasov immediately recognized the classic armored warfare strategy in motion before him, "Ah ... of course, a pincer movement. General Patton must think he can encircle them."

Bunyachenko agreed, "They will be in a position of strength to be trying such a maneuver, and they must have already achieved air-superiority to be attempting it!"

Vlasov looked at his 2IC with an optimism he hadn't shown since the war started. "*Da*, and hopefully my friend, we may be seeing some of the air cover ourselves very soon."

∞

The BlindFold shifted slightly as a startled Arjon sat up suddenly.

Atom bombs ... again?

The scene before him was one of a white-painted building in Panmunjom, North Korea. The armistice talks intended to end the Korean War had been faltering, and threatened to fail once again. The discussion around the table then took a serious turn when the United Nations delegates mentioned the use of nuclear weapons.

The armistice was signed shortly after.

∞

Znojmo, Czechoslovakia
Feb 26th, 1946

A clear blue sky welcomed the early morning sun. Golden yellow splashed onto the parapets topping the ancient stone walls of Znojmo Castle.

General Vlasov walked around the rampart overlooking the Thuya River in the valley hundreds of feet below. Across the frozen river, he spied some of the tanks and armored troop carriers of the 3rd Army's 10th Armored Division which had arrived during the night.

I expect their Commander will be here shortly ...

The previous night, the townsfolk had provided a banquet to

celebrate the linking up of the two Allied armies ... but delays in cleaning up the rear-guard units of the Red Army's 25th Guards Rifle Division, had caused the event to be postponed.

Vlasov closed his eyes and turned his face to the sun. The warmth soaked through his exhausted body, and the silence was invigorating.

Bird song had replaced the continual thump of artillery.

A lull.

It was one of those days in a war where the fleeting peace between battles was to be savored, and every minute seemed like ten.

An olive drab figure walked out on to the battlements.

Vlasov nodded approval. "Good Morning Colonel. ... I'm glad to see you made it here in one piece."

"Like-wise General," said Blackett, "although it was a rough night."

"*Da* ... we heard your fighting from here."

He raised his hand at the serenity now surrounding them. "But today is a day to be relished."

"Is Major Rhuzkoi with you?"

"Yes General, he's with Major General Bunyachenko ... exchanging details before our joint briefing this morning."

"Good," he sighed, "... there may be a respite from the war for the soldiers on the ground, but we officers do not get the day off."

The two began to pace slowly along the top of the walls, enjoying the quiet for a moment more, before Blackett said heavily, "I have news from our engagement at Linz ..."

Vlasov continued to walk steadily, but steeled himself for something he knew would be painful to hear.

"Air attacks caused the most casualties ... we had little defense against them ... we lost a lot of men."

"And when the 3rd Army ground forces attacked?" enquired the General, coming to a halt.

"Your RLA troops fought as well as could be expected under the circumstances ... we put up a token resistance and then surrendered as soon as possible."

"As expected ..." the general said softly.

Blackett shifted uncomfortably. They had all known it would be difficult, even tragic, to lose lives fighting in a battle between forces on the same side. It had been critical to stage it at the same time and in the vicinity of the 3rd Army maneuvers ... and in front of the British and French observers.

"My condolences General."

Vlasov's angst turned to steely resignation, "Accepted Colonel ... but they are not required. What we do require, Colonel Blackett, is the help of your OSS to rebuild the strength of our army."

They stood facing each other; a shared determination filled the space between the two soldiers.

"My RLA will retreat back across the Danube to regroup. With our Lend Lease equipment we will appear as just another group of Allied divisions retiring from the front lines for a rest. There we will have the prisoners taken at Linz returned to us ... but we will need more than a few thousand men to replace our losses."

Blackett's brow creased thoughtfully, *where is this going?*

"Colonel, we will need your help to recruit from the thousands who have been crossing the borders from Eastern Europe ... defectors, Cossacks, ex-Nazis ... I don't care ... as long as they hate the Bolsheviks as much as we do!"

Blackett leaned his arms on the lip of the stone parapet, thinking.

A long silence followed. Vlasov lit a cigarette and the birds seemed to sing louder.

"You've got it General. We'll get your army back to strength – I promise."

"Thank you, Colonel. It will take us many months, but we

will return to this war ... as a newly formed Russian Liberation Army."

He squared up to Blackett, his expression told of the great sacrifice his men had made in bringing events up to this point. Blackett was compelled to meet his gaze, and confirm the bond of honor that existed between them, and also between their two causes. The RLA fighting to free their homeland, and the Allies fighting to free the world.

Vlasov spoke softly but with unmistakable intent, "Our armies will fight this war together across Europe, but it will be my army that marches into Moscow to end it."

∞

But that two-handed engine at the door
Stands ready to smite once, and smite no more.
John Milton
Lycidas

Passau, Germany
March 25th, 1946

Colonel Lance Corday entered the HQ command post of his 558th Tank Destroyer Battalion and asked his staff, "Where are they?"

His officers were in a huddle, pointing and talking over the center of a map spread out on a large table.

"On the fifty-yard line sir," answered Captain Peters, pointing to a white-painted wooden marker sitting on the map – the last known forward position of their men. The highly detailed map showed Passau, a town on the Danube. The center of the town was marked with a chess piece, a black rook. The lines of elevation were compressing around the castle, and the white marker was halfway up the slope.

Making good time then, Corday thought as he focused intently on his battalion's dispositions. He glanced up from the table and scanned the interior of the building. The new command post had been set up overnight after the previous one had been hit by shellfire.

What was once a bank in the center of town was now merely a bombed-out shell. Most of the roof was still intact, however, which was why it had been selected as the new CP. The open wall-safe with its thick steel door pulled wide open, lay empty except for a layer of documents on its floor. It symbolized the state of the country they were now fighting in. Once strong and mighty, now laid waste. Its cities had been devastated by allied bombing, and then ravaged and looted by the Soviets.

Corday had spent the cool, spring morning in his jeep, touring the units at the front. The destruction was the same throughout the town, and on both sides of the river approaching Veste Oberhaus, the thirteenth-century castle overlooking the Danube.

He returned to the map. "Give me a rundown on the drive so far."

The operations officer, Captain Peters, took a breath, preparing to take point on the briefing. It meant a lot to him to make a good impression, both to his CO, and to his brother officers. His chest filled out and exuded the air of his West Point heritage.

"The Reds put up strong resistance soon after kick-off … along the road to the north of the objective … here. The division had to slow the advance a couple of times because the infantry had to clear some bunkers that the tanks had overrun."

He pointed out several key defensive points, now marked as occupied by their own troops.

"Have we confirmed the enemy units?" asked the Colonel.

"As we expected it's the 72nd Guards Rifle Division … we also suspect there is a mechanized battalion holding some T34s in reserve. We'll find out as we close in on the objective."

Corday looked up from the map, his eyes flashed expectantly

at the officers gathered around him, "I want to know *before* we find out!"

"Yes sir!" Captain Peters replied.

Peters turned to Lieutenant Clay, the intelligence officer, beside him. Clay was a bird of a different feather as demonstrated by his shoulder insignia, a black knight, which was different to the red and blue triangle of the other officers.

Captain Peters said to him, "I want eyes in the air looking for that armor ... and give me an update on weather."

As Lieutenant Clay turned and left for the Comms section, Captain Peters continued to brief the Colonel.

"Overall, the resistance has been as we anticipated ... for a rear-guard force, they put up a strong initial fight ... then fell back once we took out most of their forward artillery with air-strikes."

Colonel Corday smiled. Once again, the story was unfolding as General Patton had said it would. Air superiority was going to be the decisive factor. The tactics developed by his 3rd Army during WWII were now standard throughout the US Army. Fast, relentless, armored advances closely supported by fighter bombers and other air assets, were a devastating combination.

"What about anti-tank?" he asked.

"They've got plenty ... and we can expect more as we keep advancing."

Corday pondered for a moment, *Hmmm, still going to be a slog, even with tank-busters in the air and a mounting advantage from our own artillery. But it's gotta be done.*

He walked over to the theater map taking up most of the wall behind the tellers' counters. The lines and marks on it weren't up to date, that wouldn't happen until the General visited again. The red marks on it showed the last known position of the Soviet lines retreating across Czechoslovakia. It also showed the same colored lines in northern Germany moving forward from the states around Berlin.

Shortly after Day One, the Soviets had attacked strongly out of Brandenburg and Saxony, pushing the Allies back toward the south west. They were attempting to divide the British forces in the north-west from the Americans to the south-east. And it had been working.

The US 3rd Army had sent divisions from Czechoslovakia to shore up their western flank. That was where Corday's battalion was now fighting. All across Germany, desperate battles, costing thousands of lives had been fought to slow, and then halt the Russian advance. The outcome of the war was now hanging in the balance.

Corday stepped back from the wall, widening his view. The hill in front of them wasn't even a pin-prick on this map, and held no strategic value. This was only a mop-up operation, but it was being watched closely by the General Staff.

Corday was being given an opportunity to demonstrate new tactics with tank destroyers using a game plan he'd developed. It was one he'd worked on after a meeting with General Patton some months prior. The 3rd Army commander had made a comment about the armored divisions being the "running back" of the army. Corday had taken this analogy to an American football team, and modified it so it could be applied to another level – that of his tank destroyer battalion.

He was the offensive coach, calling the plays from the side-line, and ensuring they were executed against the enemy's defense facing his team.

He turned back to the table where Lieutenant Clay was giving the latest weather report to Captain Peters.

"We've got another recce flight in the air now. The weather'll be clearing late morning."

"Good," Peters replied. "Sir, please come over to comms, we've got a status report coming in from the hill."

They went into a large room adjacent to the bank manager's office, and gathered around one of the signalers sitting at a radio.

The operator rotated a dial to change frequency and then flicked a switch and asked in plain, "Quarterback this is Coach, what's your status? Over."

∞

Passau, Germany
Town Center
March 25th, 1946

Thunderclap concussions deafened their unprotected ears, and flying metal zipped above the helmets of a huddle of combat engineers. Pinned down by a machine-gun, the assault group was waiting for a pause in the enemy fire before making their move.

In the town, the fighting had bogged down to house to house, as the battle for Passau had gotten closer to the main bridge over the Danube leading to the castle.

Across the river from the fighting in the town, Lieutenant Deming watched through his binoculars as the assault group left cover, dashed around the corner of a house and stormed inside. One more house taken.

The reverberation of the 400hp Wright Continental engine that powered his M18 Hellcat helped to soothe his anxiety. Changing his focus to the hilltop to his left, the walled fortress of Veste Oberhaus dominated the summit. He thought it could be mistaken for the villain's castle from a medieval fairy tale.

At the battalion's current rate of progress, we should be raising the portcullis by dusk.

He searched down to his left flank, where a troop of 10th Division's T32s were firing on the dug-in defenders ahead of them. Great eruptions of flame and smoke lifted stone blocks, timber and broken bodies into the air.

The Bolsheviks responded with anti-tank gun fire, but many

of their rounds ricocheted off the 200mm frontal armor of the heavy tanks.

A puff of smoke from an anti-tank gun revealed its position as it opened fire, and rounds of 90mm HE from the T32 Grizzlies quickly silenced it.

As he watched the 50-ton giants roll on, Deming heard the voice of Corporal Ellis below him inside the turret of the tank destroyer.

"Sir, it's the Colonel. ..."

A hiss of static in his headset followed, as the call from HQ was patched through.

"Lieutenant ... how's the view over there?" asked Corday in his gruff but fatherly tone.

"Like hell sir ... for the Reds!"

Deming could picture Corday's expression, one he'd only allow for a second before hardening his focus to what lay ahead.

The colonel replied, "Well done son, keep it rolling ... I want you in the end zone before nightfall."

"You've got it sir; we're just running another play now."

While talking, he was also following the progress of the Grizzlies as they demolished another enemy position.

"We're going to push through an opening the offensive line just created."

Colonel Corday looked down at his map and frowned, "Watch your flanks ... my gut says they have armor in reserve waiting for a thrust up the center, and will try a counter-attack."

Deming grinned, "That's what we're hoping for sir ..."

The tank destroyer troop commander finished his status report with an update on the morning's casualties. He looked up. *Clear skies ... going to be a cold night.*

The castle looked even more appealing with the prospect of a warm fireplace and perhaps an intact wine cellar.

Not likely ... the Reds never leave anything behind.

"Let's get the camo net down ... we'll be moving out in five minutes," he called out to his crew.

That should give the Grizzlies enough time to regroup ... and the Reds enough time to decide where they're going to commit their tanks and counter-attack.

The tree-lined road leading up the slope would provide some cover for the troop of Hellcats. They might not be spotted until coming right up behind the Grizzlies. Surprise would be critical if they were to catch the enemy tanks at an angle.

The gunner and loader dismounted and started pulling down the camouflage netting. More hands were added to the task as several combat engineers shouldered their weapons and joined in. They'd been resting under the trees nearby, and looked as though they'd been fighting their way through hedgerows, as their uniforms and equipment were festooned with leaves and foliage.

"That'll earn you a ride for part of the way ... but not right up to the top," Deming called down to the soldiers.

"That's okay," a corporal replied. "Just drop us off at a hotel before you get there ... we'll keep watching you over the froth of our steins as you finish up!"

More soldiers back along the road took the lead of the Corporal's men, and helped uncover the other M18s in Deming's troop.

Loaded with infantry, the five Hellcats roared out from cover to exploit the breach in the Soviet defenses.

Across the Danube to the south, Colonel Corday examined the situation on the planning table before him. His tank destroyer battalion was working with Combat Command B of the 10th Armored Division. They faced units of the experienced 72nd Guards Rifle Division ... a veteran unit of the Battle of Kursk and a recipient of the Order of the Red Banner.

Although softened up by artillery and air bombardment, the enemy was giving ground slowly – too slowly for Corday's liking. He thought about his game plan. It needed momentum to succeed, just like an offensive drive in football – keep the other side off-balance. He got Captain Peters' attention.

The colonel's finger hovered over a point on the map, near the River Ilz, a tributary flowing into the Danube adjacent to Veste Oberhaus. "Here ... they'll come from here."

Captain Peters scrutinized the area. A road along the river dotted with buildings, cut through the forest. Visualizing the terrain, he worked out their possible line of approach.

"It makes sense ..." Captain Peters said. "Using the Ilz to shield their right flank. At least they'll need to come across our field of fire to get to the T32s."

"I'll make sure the spotter plane has a look along there," Lieutenant Clay added, and left for the comms room.

Corday sighed, the weight of an important decision adding gravity to his voice, "Move the TDs away from behind our medium tanks ... toward the east."

"You sure sir?" he asked respectfully. "If we're wrong, they'll be exposed and vulnerable to an attack from another vector."

Peters swept a hand over the black chess piece in the middle of the map, then along the River Ilz, "Do you think they'll try to move armor up through those trees? How can you know they won't come from another direction?"

"It's my damned job to know," said Corday, "and that area of the forest is mostly poplar and aspen ... not very thick trunks."

Lieutenant Clay returned. "Recon flight won't be over the

area for another ten minutes … they have to take a wide flight-path to avoid the ack-ack over the castle."

Corday huffed, "Never mind … it may be too late by then."

He continued with his speculation. "If we hold off the Reds' counter-attack I want a plan in place for the final push to the summit."

"Yes sir."

"We'll have done our part, and will just need to provide direct fire support for the infantry."

"Got it … the red-zone play will be ready shortly."

Captain Peters didn't think twice about having to adjust his tactics on short notice. He'd been training with Colonel Corday for the past six months. He knew everyone on the Colonel's staff was highly motivated, and on-board whenever changes in their roles were required. He started relaying new orders, and the officers around him switched to their new tasks without question. *Just like a football team*, he thought, *no one questions the coach's wisdom … just give him the information he needs about the team, or your opinion if he asks you for it.*

∞

Mojave City
2265 CE

Arjon sat back and read the newspaper headline on the screen, "Russian Spy Steals Rocket Plans."

This wasn't part of Hesta's simulation … it had really happened. He read the date on the front page of the Washington Post; January 10th, 1946. He'd been researching the corresponding timeline immediately after General Patton's accident. This story had caught his eye, so he continued reading in-depth:

"A Russian agent was arrested yesterday by the FBI. Grigori Semey, a diplomat posted to the Soviet embassy in Washington, was found to

be in possession of blueprints and other design documents for weapons captured from the Nazis by the US Army.

The stolen weapon plans included those for the dreaded V2 rocket, and for a new super-heavy tank which the German Army never got into production."

Arjon browsed through the newspapers for the following days ... protests were held around the country, largely venting anger at the Truman administration for being too soft. The Russians were getting away with huge land-grabs in Eastern Europe and in Asia. They were vocally opposed to the formation of the new United Nations, and now they were trying to steal weapons from the United States.

Hmmm ... interesting. Curious that this didn't happen in Hesta's sim.

He kept reading.

∞

Passau, Germany
March 25th, 1946

Captain Peters handed Corday the briefing notes. The colonel glanced over them quickly, as though he already knew their contents.

"Good ... consider these signed off and the new orders ready to give to Quarterback as soon the current drive plays out."

"Sir!" Peters snapped an unnecessary salute, and headed toward the comms section.

Corday removed his garrison cap and wiped his brow. These were the times he felt the heaviness of his decisions. The minutes just after he'd issued a command, were when there was time for doubt to worm itself into his thinking. Second guessing ... *had they missed anything*?

Too late now ... then it was back to dealing with the situation;

to managing the drive; to reaching the next objective.

He wished he were back in command of his tank, directing his own part of the battle from there … but those days were gone.

Since day one of the hostilities, this outfit had been morphing into something uniquely aggressive. That's why they had been given this job, cleaning out the most important salient on a line that stretched from the Baltic to Austria.

The Soviets had no significant defenses to fall back to. If they had to retreat here, they would be rolled back deep into Poland – maybe even back into Russia.

Just like the 3rd Army rolled the Nazis back into Germany from France, he thought.

Lieutenant Clay entered from comms holding a scribbled message, "We've got a sighting of armor … moving up along the Ilz."

Corday nodded, "This is it … let's hope the boys are ready."

∞

Passau, Germany
Town Center
March 25th, 1946

Black smoke, sooty and acrid from burning rubber, filled Lieutenant Deming's nostrils. While he wiped the lenses of his field glasses to remove the stringy, black particles, he glanced over his right shoulder at the source of the smoke. A store-room twenty yards away containing truck tires, was burning intensely.

From behind the cover of the smoke, he scanned the road ahead for a couple of hundred yards. Five hundred yards away, he could see Soviet infantry moving around behind a hastily prepared barricade as they set up an anti-tank gun.

So far so good, looks like they're expecting the Grizzlies to come their way.

He looked away from the road and into the bright green, spring foliage of the forest to his left.

If they're armor is coming along-side the Ilz river, they'll be hoping to outflank their tanks ... but instead we'll be ...

He held his breath. *Did that tree just move?*

Out of the corner of his eye he then saw the top of another tree waver, then crash forward.

"Load AP!"

Another tree was flattened, this time it crashed down onto the road.

"Target front! Three hundred!"

A dark green shape lumbered out on to the road, branches and shattered greenery splayed all around it.

"FIRE!"

The 90mm tungsten core shell slammed into the Soviet tank's soft side armor and it exploded into flame.

More T34s spilled out onto the road.

Deming ducked down into the open-topped turret of the Hellcat, knowing what was coming next. A cannonade blasted through the air as the other four M18s lined up along the road behind them opened fire.

The tank-destroyers lived up to their name. Two more burning wrecks didn't make it across the road. Two of the T34s did, and several more stopped short and stayed in the trees.

The lead Hellcat's crew let out a whoop, allowing themselves to celebrate a well-executed ambush. The smoke had provided a perfect cover ... all they'd had to do while lying in wait, was fix their sights along the road so as not to rely on clear visibility when firing at their targets.

"Let's move!" Deming called over the radio to his troop. There were too many Soviet tanks for them to handle without support. At least the ambush would have slowed them down, and made them think twice about continuing toward the exposed flank of the main body of US armor.

They left the main road and turned down a dirt track to the right, back toward the last known position of the Grizzlies.

Deming kept glancing back over his shoulder to see if any of the enemy tanks were following, but he knew they wouldn't be able to keep up with the M18s. With a top speed of fifty miles per hour, the Hellcat was the fastest armored vehicle around.

The troop slowed up after a couple of miles. As they idled slowly through a group of houses scattered along either side of the dirt road, Deming crouched down lower into his seat. The crews had to be watchful of second floor windows. A concealed machine-gun could wreak havoc on the men inside the open turrets of the M18s.

Passing slowly out of the houses, the forest returned. Through the trees, Deming could see the tops of the stone ramparts of the castle.

Better get moving ... if I can see them, they can see me.

As though on cue, the loud crack of a 40mm shell screamed through the air over their heads. It exploded behind them, demolishing the front porch of one of the houses.

The lead M18 halted, while the four behind split off to both sides of the track and sought cover in the trees. Deming spied a puff of smoke curling out of the doorway on the side of an old brick building.

"Load HE!"

"Target – two o'clock!"

His heartbeat pounded in his ears ... the enemy would need fifteen seconds to reload. Below him, the barrel of the 90mm gun swung in an agonizingly slow arc, "House – ground floor ..."

Six ... five ... four ...

The barrel stopped moving. "Fire!"

The house collapsed in a maelstrom of high explosive, turning it into a waterfall of smoking flame and dust. The sounds of crumbling masonry and splintered wood reached the ears of the M18's crew.

No celebration this time ... that had been too close. They would need to be more careful moving through the forest to join up with Combat Command B.

Deming waved the troop on.

Fifteen minutes later, they sighted the Grizzlies, now at the base of the slope leading up to Veste Oberhaus. Deming called a halt, needing to appraise the situation and determine where to deploy his tank destroyers to provide the best support. He waved directions to his troop, spreading them out along a low rise in hull down position.

Deming put in a call to HQ and confirmed their orders.

The battle for the lower slopes continued in earnest, with heavy casualties being suffered on both sides. From the north-west, another troop of Hellcats approached – the rest of Deming's platoon.

"Get the troop to switch to the platoon frequency," he ordered the radio operator. He waited a moment for the others to switch, then picked up his radio handset.

"We wait here until those T34s show up," he called to the other M18 commanders. The eight tank destroyers would need to protect the main force's left. Within minutes, a company of combat engineers arrived to support them.

The column of half-tracks, some towing guns, raced up and spread out between the M18s. The engineers jumped out and quickly set up their anti-tank weapons.

They didn't have to wait long.

The Soviet tanks, now followed by massed infantry, swarmed through the trees, heading for the US forces attacking the castle.

Deming watched patiently. They would hold their fire until each M18 was certain of its target. A haggard looking captain commanding the combat engineers called up to him, wanting to know when they should open fire.

"What happens next?" the engineer Captain asked.

Deming answered in his mid-western drawl. "Those are tanks ... these are tank-destroyers ... what do you think's going to happen?"

Artillery rounds and rockets started landing across the battlefield. It was being fired from the vicinity of the castle. The Allied artillery stayed silent – the Americans wouldn't risk hitting their own men. The Bolsheviks weren't so discriminating.

The other M18 commanders had selected their targets – Deming raised his arm, also nodding to the Captain who was still watching. His arm dropped.

A hellish scene followed. The Soviet tanks and infantry were side-on to the Hellcats and anti-tank guns. Three T34s went up in flames.

As the M18s reloaded, Deming opened up with the .50 cal.

The thumping sound of the machine gun was suddenly drowned out as one of the half-tracks, an anti-aircraft M16 with quad-50 cals, started firing at the infantry around the T34s. The effect on the advancing infantry was devastating. Bodies were torn apart by the ferocious impacts from the heavy machine guns.

The Red Army counter-attack faltered. A few tanks changed direction and headed toward the tank destroyers on the rise. At the same time, the Russian artillery fire began to close in on them. The Americans had revealed their position when they opened fire – and had now been spotted by the OP in the castle.

A rising wail met Deming's ears. His heart stopped as the sound approached with steam-engine certainty.

"Back off! Back off!" he shouted to his driver.

The Hellcat's engine roared and it lurched back down the slope as a massive crack of doom sounded. The AA half-track disintegrated from a direct hit by the artillery, instantly killing its crew.

Another wail approached. Screaming louder than the last volley. Deming recognized it as the sound of a rocket barrage fired from a Katyusha. The top of the slope began erupting with explosion after explosion. He looked around to see his troop following his lead and backing away from the rise. That was his last thought before the world flew upside down.

∞

Mojave City
2265 CE

"Hesta, now show me the headlines from the New York Times, January 24th, 1946 – not from your matrix – the real ones," asked Arjon.

"REDS DENIED ATOM BOMB!"

"A Soviet spy network has been uncovered with links to Great Britain and its atomic weapons program. The network was plotting to pass on top secret details gained from a British physicist working on the Allied atomic bomb program, also known as the Manhattan Project, to the Kremlin.

The physicist, Klaus Fuchs, has been detained and charged with espionage, and is awaiting trial in the United States."

So, thought Arjon, *in reality the communists had been thwarted in their attempts to steal the plans for the atomic bomb – but in Hesta's matrix they had succeeded.*

"Hesta ... why do think this event did not occur in your simulation?" Arjon asked.

"The probability matrix cannot provide a fully audited breakdown of specific causality leading to a deterministic outcome."

"You mean you don't know?"

"Correct."

"But can we infer that the war against the Soviets led to a tighter security regime in US research installations, and that led to the failure of the plot to steal the atom bomb?"

"That assumption can be deduced from the high-level streams of the event continuity."

"Thank you, go back to sleep."

∞

Passau, Germany
March 25th, 1946

Colonel Corday took the message slip from Lieutenant Clay and after reading it to himself, held it up to get his staff officers' attention.

He then read aloud, "Quarterback sacked ... platoon engaging enemy armor counter-attacking from east of Veste Oberhaus."

"Who's in command?" asked Captain Peters.

"The signal is from Lieutenant Ellery ... the platoon 2IC," said Colonel Corday as he crumpled the message.

Taking only a few seconds to compose himself and show a determined resolve to his officers, he added, "They have to hold their ground."

He scoured the map table, "Move up the reserve units –

Lieutenant Jarrett's recon outfit has two mobile artillery and some mechanized infantry. They can bolster Ellery's position."

"Have them move up before nightfall." Although clearly disappointed with the situation – the commander out of action, and the threat of the Reds pushing them back down the hill – he still sounded resolute.

"We'll beat off this attack, but we'll have to delay the final push on the hill until we've regrouped."

∞

Mojave City
2265 CE

Arjon was becoming almost obsessive as he kept reading about the simulation's alternative past, and then switching to the same time period in his own history for comparison.

He read another newspaper headline from the real Washington Post, this time from March 25th, 1946:

"MARINES LAND IN POLAND!"

"The United States 1st Marine Corp has successfully landed behind the Russian front lines and taken the strategic port of Gdansk. In a statement released this morning, General MacArthur said that the '… landings have achieved all of their initial objectives, and have given us, and our allies, a major seaport from which to launch further advances.'"

∞

Passau, Germany
March 26th, 1946

The grogginess returned and clouded Lieutenant Deming's focus. He willed himself to snap out of it. Colonel Corday had said something to him ... *hope that wasn't important.*

He thought the row of newly delivered M18s looked out of place. Painted with olive green and brown camouflage ready for the approaching summer, they glowed under a coat of dew in the morning sun.

Nothing else in the ordnance depot looked as shiny and new. It was as if something so clean and untried couldn't be trusted out on the battlefield.

Corday's voice filtered its way through those of the birds calling out in the trees above.

"... now has wider tracks ... twenty-one inches, to handle the extra weight. They had to counter the additional recoil from the higher caliber gun ..."

Deming nodded and wiped his brow. A smear of blood smudged across his forehead as he adjusted his bandage. The Colonel's voice was harmonizing with the birdsong, threatening to lull him further into his daze.

"... and the engineers at GM have upgraded the hydramatic transmission."

Corday looked at his junior staffer. "You ok?"

Deming just nodded, as if the effort of speaking would cause him to lose his concentration and the technical detail would not be absorbed.

"When they tested the new transmission, they staged a race with a Jeep," said Corday enthusiastically.

"From a standing start ... over three hundred feet."

Corday exuded the status of a privileged messenger as he looked Corday in the eye.

"An eighteen-ton tank against a one-ton jeep ... the Hellcat won. Did it under sixteen seconds."

Deming whistled. "Shoot ... but it doesn't surprise me sir. They've got so much torque, we get those tanks moving back and forth like they're rocking horses."

With the fuzziness in his head clearing, he moved up to pat

the 105mm short-barreled howitzer and asked, "What about angled penetration?"

"The 105mm HEAT rounds have a shaped charge ... that means you've got to get as close to ninety degrees as possible or it won't get through, the same as regular AP."

"No problem on their square turrets then ... just gonna need to be spot on when we're aiming at their soup bowls."

"Right. The gunners should avoid targeting the sloped turret armor on their latest IS models unless you've got some advantage from elevation."

"Hmmm ... always get the high ground. Holds as true as it ever did."

"The rest of your platoon's M18s are going to be issued with the latest high-velocity AP ammunition for their 90-millimeters. The new HVAP rounds will go through 300mm of armor at 500 yards."

Deming whistled again. "Whew! That's gonna dish out some pain ... the boys'll want to run into one of those new IS3s *a* ... *s* ... *a* ... *p* to see what they can do."

The effort of being so positive took its toll. Deming concentrated hard, closing his eyes hoping that would keep the persistent headache at bay. The blackness in his mind was suddenly interrupted by a vivid memory of his Hellcat being lifted into the air by the explosion, and himself being thrown out of the open turret and slammed into the ground like a toy soldier.

Corday noticed his discomfort but continued anyway, "Now ... all this talk of firepower is fine – but it won't be our weaponry that wins this war."

Deming nodded through the pain to show he was still paying attention. He suppressed a wince as he saw the M18 burst into flames ... his crew still inside.

He willed himself to snap out of it as he realized he was about to hear one of his CO's pep talks.

"Tanks, guns and planes all need someone to use them ... and we use them more effectively than any other army."

Deming's spirits lifted. *Now that I can relate to.*

"I agree sir." he responded, "We've had our initiation under fire … ever since Torch in '43 we've had to make the best of inferior armor against the Nazis."

"Damn right, and we've had to be better soldiers to beat them."

Corday relaxed a little, satisfied that his top platoon leader, although a casualty of their last skirmish, Deming had come through mentally unscathed. He'd been grooming him for higher command, and now knew that the man standing alongside him was the right one for the job.

"Lieutenant, I'm promoting you to Captain," he said, still watching Deming's responses carefully.

"Why, thank you, sir … I'm very honored."

"And I want you to know I've got you tagged for higher command."

"I won't let you down."

"As you know, my battalion doesn't follow traditional command structures. My game plans are described as 'innovative' by the top brass … and the army doesn't readily accept change or a new idea without grinding it through a mill, and tempering it until they know it's strong enough to work."

Corday led them off at an easy walk. "My plans are getting results, so I'll continue to get the leeway I need to keep shaping this unit."

Deming no longer noticed the ache in his head as he fell in stride with the Colonel. He felt as if he were now being privileged to a new level of the senior officer's confidence as he detailed the battalion's future direction.

"Other tank destroyer battalions usually get their companies divided amongst the armored divisions. They mostly get assigned to defensive missions, supporting infantry, and dealing with counter attacks."

The trees became silent, the chorus of bird life subsiding

as though granting Corday's words the sole right to resound through the chill morning air.

"I'm going to use the Hellcats for what they were intended to do ... to destroy large numbers of tanks!"

"Yes sir! There's sure gonna be plenty of them!"

"Bet your ass there will ..."

An adjutant came out of one of the HQ's out-buildings with two cups of coffee.

The two officers stood for a moment, sipping from steaming mugs, and looking back to the line of Hellcats.

"Those are the most mobile armored vehicles in the European theater," Corday said flatly.

"Yeah ... we've got fifty miles an hour out of 'em on firm ground."

"And the Reds get at best thirty-seven out of an IS2 – and that's if it's going downhill. The M18s got the firepower to handle the heaviest tanks the Reds have got."

"Thirty-seven hundred feet per second muzzle velocity on the upgraded 90mm guns – it does the job if it's used correctly."

"Well, we're going to be using them in a tactically modified role that will at first *not* be appreciated by the followers of established tank destroyer doctrine."

They walked on, talking tactics as the air began to warm, carrying with it a scent of the summer to come. The season for finishing a war.

∞

Liberty, equality and democracy are the inalienable right of all human beings. It is the responsibility of the organization to ensure the rights of the individual are unimpeded by the laws or practices of any of the nations of Earth.
Article 42
Charter of the Union of Nations

"Holo-park?" asked Eya.

"Maybe not, they'll be here in a couple of hours. I'm just going to take a shower," Arjon replied as he came out of his den.

Paradise may have provided for all human needs and wants, but one deficiency remained constant – time.

He sighed at the thought of missing another session at the park. His personal projects had kept him away for another week, and the drone-ball team would give him a ribbing once he returned. Apart from the exercise, it was camaraderie he missed the most.

He entered the shower and as the jets of water washed away his frustration, he felt virtual hands pressing deeply as they rolled over his muscles. The sonic masseur would at least help him maintain his fitness. He relaxed completely and bowed his head as the light pressure from the sub-sonic sound waves focused on a knot of tension above his scapula, then gently strengthened to iron it out.

An hour later, as a warm evening breeze wafted in from the Mojave, the bower echoed with the sound of clinking glasses and voices rising to be heard.

Ah, a successful dinner party, thought Eya. *Half a dozen of our best friends ... and no stressed-out hosts.*

She handed her empty plate to the robo-serve as it meandered past on its way to the kitchen, and carefully placed her used cutlery in a padded receptacle in the robot's midriff. She was particularly proud of the tableware – a wedding present from Arjon. It was made from titanium mined from the asteroid belt.

"The desserts will now be served!" she announced.

Heads turned with the sounds of swooning over the array of pastries, fresh cream and chocolate dishes. And the centerpiece, a huge cornucopia of fruit grown on the space stations in high orbit above Earth. The exaggerated shapes, sizes and colors resulting from growing in low gravity gave the display the look of a surrealist masterpiece.

Arjon smiled at Eya. He'd wanted everyone's tastes to be well satisfied at this party, so they'd be in a good mood for the game they were going to play later on.

The guests didn't need to make the effort of choosing. Hesta could detect everyone's preferences from their expressions and biometric data as they savored the fare. She relayed instructions to the robo-serve and it dutifully began to give everyone what they wanted.

Thus, the conversation flowed without interruption.

"The mind is the temple of the soul!" Macrose almost shouted, slapping the table at the same time an artificial hand retrieved his dinner plate.

"Oh, that's fine ... if you like temples," quipped Grillon. "I prefer to think of mine as more of a wine cellar."

"Whether it's in a temple, or a cellar ..." said Eya, "I think we've exhausted the whole *'soul actually does exist'* topic."

"I agree," added Arjon, "and for a change from our

metaphysical discussions, I have a little game for us to play after dessert. It's called 'Alternative Reality.'"

Hesta took her cue and materialized a holo-card in front of each guest.

The information on the front of each one was biometrically tuned to only become visible when it was sensed that the owner of the card was looking at it, and so it would only be seen by them.

Arjon explained, "We each take turns giving a clue from our cards, which is a description of a scenario, or feature from our alternative world. It also lists an event that occurred in our other world, that is related to that clue. So, once we hear the clue, the others have to try and guess what the event is that caused it."

"Oh, I'm way too high for this game!" said Margeaux.

"That's alright Margie, you're allowed to use your hand-held to think of answers for you!" said Eya.

After a few minutes more of explaining the rules, Arjon started the game.

∞

Passau, Germany
March 30th, 1946

Captain Deming shifted uncomfortably, feeling out of place. The 10th Armored Division HQ was alive with activity. Officers, mostly strangers to him, huddled over maps making adjustments to unit movements already in place. Signalmen carried messages back and forth to the comms section, and at the head of the large rectangular map table Colonel Corday stood alongside the division commander, Major General Wyatt.

Deming thought they looked like two statues, isolated and still among the apparent disorder. Despite the commotion, if either of them had uttered a word for the others to hear, the room would have come to a standstill.

He stretched his arms, feeling the acute ache from his bruises. At least the effects from the concussion were easing. Stretching didn't help; at least he was on a light duty schedule, here only to observe the Division's operations center, but not having any direct involvement was presenting a challenge to his powers of concentration.

Corday's 558th tank destroyer battalion had had been attacking since dawn, in cooperation with several of the Divisions' tank-infantry units. It was a good thing the Red Army units ahead of them had been cut off, otherwise they would have had time to strengthen their position with fresh troops – as they always did.

Deming spotted a black chess piece on the map table – Corday's staff must have brought it from the 558th HQ to the division HQ for the final coordinated push.

He also spotted one of the officers from the 558th around the map table – Captain Peters. The captain straightened and got the colonel's attention.

"Sir, red-zone play is ready to start."

"About time," Corday snapped. "The light's fading."

The previous days had been spent holding off repeated Russian counter-attacks, the last of which had finally been broken after the timely arrival of a squadron of fighter bombers. Air support for the ground offensive was in high demand across the entire front, and would usually only turn up at the most crucial moments.

Over the following hour, the sounds and reverberations of the battle increased, reaching them through the walls and floor from a few miles away. Deming felt a mix of anxiety and exhilaration at the thought of his platoon fighting on the slopes below the castle. He had frequently had to resist an urge to go outside, as though being under the same gray-blue sky as his men would bring him closer to them.

Corday asked the Captain for a progress report.

"It seems the Soviet resistance is finally waning sir. We're seeing multiple break-throughs and forward units are closing on the summit," Captain Peters advised.

This morning's counter-attack must have been a last-ditch effort … thought Deming. *This is all going to be over soon.*

He finally allowed himself to leave the room, and went outside. The heaviness in his head soon lightened as he walked out into the brisk early evening air.

The echoing call of the battle on the hill was diminishing, a drum roll of gunfire slowing to the fading thump of a heartbeat. He could see a wide column of smoke above the parapets of Veste Oberhaus, and orange flashes showing where the last desperate infantry fire-fights were concluding.

A hand patted him on the shoulder. It was Colonel Corday's.

"Don't worry son, your unit did a fine job … you'll be back with them soon."

Deming looked him in the eye. The look they shared was one of men who'd been in combat. It told of loss and of victory at the same time, and of the expectation for more the next day. And then again after that.

As the two watched the surreal bonfire around the distant castle, words did not seem appropriate. The situation allowed Deming to see something in Corday that he hadn't seen before. An anguish that was a result of this kind of remoteness, of being part of a battle on a hill miles away, but knowing that the impact of the decisions they made down here had consequences – severe consequences, for those up on the hill.

Darkness closed around the town, and Veste Oberhaus, beneath its great pillar of smoke – the city's headstone, fell silent. Corday and Deming walked back into the command post. Deming stopped just inside the doorway, and looked on as Colonel Corday continued up to the table and reached out his hand. The entire staff watched him as he picked up the black chess piece in the center, and let then let the rook topple over to lay fallen on its side.

Game over.

∞

The quest for virtue begins with our children. If not found, society's
example must lead the way.
Mantra of the Continuation
Bureau of Sanity

"A company wants to mine an asteroid for its precious metals, but they have to wait seven years for the paperwork to be processed," Margeaux read from her holo-card.

"Mmmm ... sounds like the Space Resources Council has adopted a public service model ..." said Macrose.

"Clearly the restrictions of some kind of socialist bureaucracy are being imposed upon free-enterprise," said Grillon with incredulity.

"The asteroid's trajectory will take it beyond a financially viable distance for exploitation in two years ... there is no avenue for appeal," added Margeaux.

"Communists!" Macrose spat vehemently.

"There obviously isn't an SRC, so outer space is finders-keepers," Tomass pointed out, "That would explain why such a draconian regulatory body has come into existence."

"Correct!" Margeaux almost shouted with relief. She had been getting worried that her clues weren't good enough and no one would be able to guess the answer.

"Hesta, elaborate for us," asked Arjon.

"The current global entity known as the Space Resources Council does not exist, and its intended function of providing an efficient administrative process for the exploitation of extra-terrestrial resources is performed by each nation's own governing body."

"Madness ..." said Grillon. "Years of pussy-footing around to make sure a company operating in your country's jurisdiction doesn't file a competing claim with that of another country ..."

Arjon followed up by asking Hesta, "How would disagreements over claims be addressed?"

"The matrix extrapolates a ninety-four percent chance of military conflict between nations occurring as a result of unresolved territorial disputes."

Macrose picked up his glass and said sarcastically, "A toast ... to perpetual conflict!"

"First the solar system ... then the galaxy!" said Grillon as he clinked glasses with Macrose.

"Now you can see how all this carefree living is making us go soft," Macrose said sarcastically. "Outer-space is the last frontier that humanity has where we can fight each other with some justification."

He picked up his shiny titanium fork and turned it over in his hand. "And think of the economic activity that would be generated by the need for military hardware that allows us to kill each other in zero-G."

∞

A system of government which requires that all individuals serve the state will stifle personal freedom and hence perpetuate negativity. It will foster a culture that breeds tyranny, and result in a society undermined by innate hostility and resentment. By default, that hostility will be directed toward cultures that embrace freedom.
Section D of Submission by Bureau of Sanity: Criteria for Amending the Mandate for the Security Council of the Union of Nations

∞

April 21st, 1946
Bialystok, Poland

Dust skidded up around the wheels of a Douglas C-47 transport plane as it touched down on a compacted clay runway.

Another uneventful flight, thought General Patton as he looked out at the temporary prefab buildings and supply dumps, and unbuckled his safety-belt. He felt gratified that no fighter escort had been necessary for the flight from Warsaw to the front lines.

Their role is almost entirely ground support now that the Red air force has been reduced to a purely defensive role.

An airman deployed the ladder from the waist door, and then snapped to attention as the VIP passenger stepped down. The general returned the airman's salute, standing for a moment, and considering the unforgiving hardness of the ground beneath his feet. Sniffing the air, he noticed a hint of morning dampness lacing the otherwise clear, crispness of spring.

Not as dry as the capital, he mused, turning his thoughts back to the conference at US East European Command, *but a helluva lot drier than where the Russkies are sitting.* The USEEC conference had been well timed, during a week's lull in the fighting which had allowed the rapidly advancing Allied armies to straighten their lines, and consolidate their supply situation.

Patton's staff were still in Warsaw, formalizing the strategic decisions made at the conference, so he had taken the flight back to the front alone. His solitude had allowed him to reflect on the big picture. What a difference from the years of war against the Nazis and the Japanese. The top military leadership was doing what it was meant to do: lead. The politicians were in the back rows, not on center stage. Why? The horror and atrocities of the war had been fully disclosed, and the blame for those political and cultural genocides laid squarely where they belonged – with corrupted leaders and their self-serving ideologies. Leaders such as Hitler, Mussolini ... and Stalin. Not the military.

Generals such as Patton and MacArthur, were the first to proclaim that an alternative solution to violent conflict should always be sought, and that war should be a last resort.

The media and political campaign espousing the danger to world peace posed by communism, for which Patton had been the figurehead, had resulted in a double benefit: both to initiate the resumption of war production, and also to produce a shift in the internal balance of power.

In this war, the Allied military were not serving individual nations, but an ideal: the Free World. A union of countries committed to preventing war being used as a means of resolving human conflicts, and finally ending tyranny.

And now, after the initial bitter fighting in Germany and Czechoslovakia, the war was rolling north-east. As expected, the central plains of Poland had seen only slight resistance, and delaying tactics from the retreating Soviets. Patton knew, though, that they would be concentrating their defenses along the Russian border, and here ... at Bialystok.

Third Army was poised to spearhead the offensive that would follow the same route as that taken by the Nazis five years earlier. A line through Minsk, Smolensk and finally to Moscow.

Patton was a firm believer in studying the roads and routes taken during previous conquests. Even though the Germans had not succeeded in taking the Russian capital, the lightning advance of 1941's Operation Barbarossa across the steppes had been no fluke. During the conference in Warsaw he'd made a point of pointing out the German precedent to many British and French commanding generals.

A broad smile crossed his aquiline features, a moment of reflected satisfaction with his work at highest strategic levels. The allies were stronger now than they had ever been. The flow of arms and máteriel that had previously crossed the Atlantic to Russia under the Lend-Lease agreement, were now going to the French and British.

The irony was delicious.

The Dodge command car that had been waiting for him took him away from the airfield, and shortly after headed out onto a sealed highway. As they accelerated along the road, Patton noticed a column of slower moving vehicles ahead. Dozens of trucks laden with supplies were being held up by even slower-moving armor.

The driver didn't slow down as they swung out to overtake, almost straddling the verge on the other side of the road. As the tail-end vehicles dropped behind them, Patton saw that the armor holding up the supply column was comprised of the weapon platform that was going to break through the toughest Red Army fortifications: the T95.

Being carried aboard its specially built Thornycroft tank transporter, the massively armored T95 weighed 86 tons. It had a top speed of just eight miles per hour, and as such was hardly capable of reaching the battlefield under its own steam. Patton chuckled inside as he admired the metal beast laying dormant on its trailer. He thought it resembled a cold-blooded crocodile, basking in the sun and soaking up the energy it would soon need. *No wonder the GIs nicknamed it the Leatherjacket.*

He sat back and allowed himself to feel some satisfaction. The fruits of his constant harassment and cajoling of politicians to get his soldiers the best weaponry ever produced, was on its way with him to the front line.

∞

General Patton arrived at 10th Armored Division HQ around midday. As he stepped out of his staff car he looked around with some concern at the location chosen for the headquarters. The Renaissance architecture of Hasbach Palace although admirable, was not his preferred choice for a command center. A less conspicuous site would have been more appropriate. Perhaps

Major General Wyatt had confidence that the air was still under the complete control of the Allied air-forces.

He walked toward the main entrance as Major General Hyram Wyatt came outside to meet him. They snapped their hands to the brims of their hats, and then shook hands.

"General … I see the skies are very clear around here," said Patton drily, looking up at the azure blue day.

They went inside and the HQ staff stood at attention, holding their salutes until the 3rd Army Commander returned theirs.

"Gentlemen, thank you for the warm reception," he said with sincerity. "And now, let's work out how we're going to kick the Reds back to the Stone Age where they belong."

The operations staff returned to their duties as Patton, Wyatt, and Colonel Corday retired to Wyatt's office.

Inside, Patton took a chair at the head of a small conference table, "Well Hyram, you'll be pleased to know that the replacement armor is only an hour behind me."

Wyatt and Corday smiled at each other.

Patton continued, "As I promised, your division will receive the lion's share of the new T30s."

"… and the T95s?" Wyatt asked expectantly.

"On the way … slowly," said Patton. He leaned forward and pointed to a tacked line on the map before them.

"This railroad system will be critical to us for the advance on Moscow."

His expression was pained with frustration. "It'll be needed to bring up the weaponry such as the T95s we'll be using to reduce the heaviest Russian fortifications."

Wyatt thought for a moment about the new motor gun carriage with one-foot thick frontal armor – so thick it would withstand a direct hit from the highest caliber Soviet anti-tank guns. A logistical nightmare, but ultimately they were going to be worth the effort to get them to the front line. As he was thinking about how they were going to be integrated into his division's structure, he kept an ear open as General Patton continued.

"I've seen them in action at Aberdeen ... they'll be breaking through bunker systems without stopping. Their 105s' fire rounds are particularly effective against concrete."

He sighed, clearly frustrated at having such an immobile tank in his cavalry, then pounded a fist on the table, "... but they're so goddammed slow it's infuriating!"

Corday agreed, "Yes General, it'll be a different kind of offensive to the one we prefer ... until we make a break-through."

Patton scrutinized the Colonel with a shrewd look, "Why Colonel, I believe there's a reason your battalion is the new favorite in my Army ... hitting the enemy hard and fast, and then keep on moving."

"Yes sir!" Corday's eyes flashed with enthusiasm for the fighting ahead. "And our Hellcat's have been working on being even *more* mobile in their exercises designed for the terrain approaching Minsk."

Wyatt scanned the map, aware of the importance of neutralizing the Red Army forces around Bialystok in order to achieve the objective of capturing the rail systems around Minsk.

"With regard to the coordination with air support ... I assume they will be hitting their trains and leaving the junctions intact?"

"Correct. They rebuild the lines anyway so it's a low-value target. Fighter bombers will be concentrating on destroying the supply trains themselves rather than just cutting the line and impeding their progress temporarily. Heavy bombing targets will be focusing on their production infrastructure, such as tank and munitions factories."

Patton stood up and went to a larger wall map, "Timing is the key factor. Right now, the Red Army supply lines are wallowing in the spring thaw."

His cane roved through the air in front of the map, pointing out areas to the north of the front, where the effects of the snow-melt were much greater than on their own supply routes.

"Rivers are flooding and the roads are impassable. If we move too soon, we'll get bogged down in the same mud."

His cane moved to Kiev in the south. "In the next two weeks, we will be moving our reserves up from the Ukraine where we are holding strongly."

He traced a line from Kiev, up through Minsk, then on to the Baltic states, where the tip of the cane rested on the seaport of Riga.

"The Marines' advance in the north-west is moving rapidly, so the Reds are consolidating a defensive line which focuses on their center ..." again the cane swept over the map as though it were an instrument of destiny being wielded by a demi-god, "here, around Minsk."

Patton moved back to the smaller map on the table, one which detailed the immediate area to their front.

"Our reserves from the south will cross into Belorussia to coincide with our upcoming offensive. To the Russians' credit, they don't rely on static fortifications like Maginot or Siegfried ... but from our recon we know they are preparing a deep defensive concentration forward of Minsk, similar to their response against the Nazi's Operation Citadel at Kursk. That's where we'll have to focus our initial attack."

Colonel Corday finally saw an opportunity to speak up. "Sir ... this situation in the center seems ideal for a new strategy I'd like to present to you."

Patton looked at General Wyatt, who nodded affirmatively.

"Go ahead ... I'm always open to operational initiatives ... as long as they're going to align with a philosophy of hitting-hard, and then keep moving."

"It does sir."

Corday went to a blackboard and picked up a piece of white chalk.

"My tank destroyer battalion has been conducting exercises which are not standard TD doctrine."

He drew a horizontal line across the middle of the board, then a large arrow pointing upwards and dissecting the line at the center.

"As we break through their defensive line, our armored spearhead needs to keep moving fast to exploit that breach."

Patton listened quietly, recognizing his own strategy being demonstrated.

"The Russian defenses will be very concentrated. Too concentrated for us to just ignore, so we would normally have to slow down to mop up ... then resume the advance."

"I'm listening," said Patton.

"My tank destroyers, together with support from combat engineers, can provide a 'mobile defense' for our fast-moving armored advance."

He drew a series of smaller arrow heads leading off the large one, like branches on a cactus.

"We can rapidly deploy to negate any threat to our rear posed by counter-attacks sourced from those defensive positions we leave behind."

Corday paused, seeing that Patton was thinking intently. The General's eyes glowed with a restrained fire, then blazed suddenly as he decided he liked what he was hearing.

"Go on ... I can see you may have something that will keep the advance moving faster ... I want to hear more."

Corday also looked to General Wyatt, after all, it would be his armored division that would be signing up for the new strategy. Wyatt nodded his approval, so Corday continued.

"Tank destroyers have traditionally been used as a defensive element, being held back in case an enemy counter-attack breaks through our lines and we have to deal with their armor."

Corday lamented how his battalion had been used in the past, then added fervently, "My Hellcats are a fast-moving armored vehicle. We should use that mobility to advantage ... by having them constantly on the move just behind the very forward armored units."

He stroked out more arrows on the board, "As the enemy tries to hit our armored columns from the flank or even our rear, we can protect them by repelling those counter-attacks and then quickly resume our position behind the main advance."

Patton agreed, "We'll bring this into our overall planning … General Wyatt if you'll arrange a briefing with my staff this week it would be much appreciated."

The 3rd Army commander thought for a moment, then asked Corday, "Where did these ideas come from?"

Corday, already enthusiastic at being able to present his plan to one of the greatest generals of the war, was now euphoric, "Why … it was inspired from something you once said sir … from a football analogy, about the armored division being the running back of the team."

Patton chuffed, "Yes, the running back. So how do tank destroyers fit in to that picture?"

"With due respect sir, the mobile defense provided by the tank destroyers will add to that concept … by giving the running back some defensive accountability … I call it the Blocking Running Back."

"Ahhh … of course! The running back that blocks any moves from the defensive team … giving the quarter back more time to keep the drive going – interesting."

Wyatt shook his head at the two, wondering how this was going to affect his division. He'd gone along with Corday's ideas before as they'd been so effective, but in isolation. Now the Colonel had Patton's ear, and those ideas were going to be influencing his entire division directly. He felt he should remind the other two, still talking excitedly about football, that their decisions would have consequences in the real world – in a real war.

As though to symbolize his perspective, and that of the division, he reached into a drawer beneath the table and picked out an object. Placing it on Minsk with a loud thud the other two would hear, he said, "And so we prepare to storm the next castle … into the breach dear friends."

On the map, the objective now lay marked in readiness for the 10th Armored … with the black rook.

∞

Mojave City
2265 CE

Rilith read from her holo-card. "The Soviets exercise their veto in the United Nations Security Council which prevents the policing of nations who are claiming disputed territory within the Arctic Circle. The North Polar War begins in 2023."

"Qwerty! Another war …" said Lorman, Rilith's date, "… I don't think this game is going to last much longer."

"Oh, why not?" asked Eya.

Lorman looked at his hostess like a serpent coiling around its prey, "Surely this alternative world is going to destroy itself? Or be destroyed … because its people are so focused on the business of killing each other that they're going to miss developing some crucial piece of technology … one that will be needed to defend themselves?"

"Defend themselves … against what?" asked Arjon, pouring a faintly glowing purple liqueur into his glass.

Lorman thought for a moment, then smiled with satisfaction as though his prey were about to be devoured, "Oh, remember that asteroid in the news about twenty years ago, the big one with a composition similar to stainless steel?"

"Yes!" added Macrose, "It was named *Amen2248* because it was on a collision course with the Earth." Then he added thoughtfully, "Because of its size and mass, didn't we have to use some kind of kinetic energy mechanism to change its trajectory?"

"Yes ... multiple kinetic drives installed on its surface months in advance," answered Grillon, and then his tone dropped down an octave, "... or else it would have hit us with the equivalent of a million-megaton impact. The End."

Arjon could feel the effects of the liqueur washing over him. Picking up the bottle, he read aloud from the label. "A nectar sourced from the moment sunlight and chlorophyll were destined to meet. The heat and humidity of the Colombian jungle summon forth a resin of mystical potency from only the purest sinsemilla." He smiled at his guests.

"Weed! Who brought a cannabis liqueur?" he asked in an amused tone.

Macrose owned up. "Oh, now Arjon don't be a fuddy-duddy. It's been legal everywhere for over a century."

Arjon just shrugged, becoming intensely interested in the violet glow swirling around in his liqueur glass.

His thoughts wandered. Asteroid impacts, world wars ... tyranny and oppression. He could see the tragic and simply turn it into the ridiculous.

The Alternative Reality game had become a kind of psychotherapy session. He looked at his beautiful wife surrounded by their wonderful friends. Then he thought of the matrix and its world of alternative madness.

He realized that he and Eya had been suffering from an insidious lament. Their carefree and blissful happiness had been undermined by depression and anxiety – the result of the enhanced emotional impact from experiencing the enacted global events of the matrix.

He watched Eya laughing and smiling, and realized that being able to laugh and mock the matrix's claims was having a healing effect on them both.

Macrose, as was his way, brought a competitive element back to the game. "Forget about the meteorite apocalypse ... you still haven't guessed why the polar bears became extinct."

"Because all those explosions in the Polar War melted the ice?" Rilith offered meekly.

"Good try ..." said Macrose.

Grillon tried to explain a pattern he could see emerging. "It seems there's a common theme here ... that an ineffective *United* Nations – note the name change ... is a major influence on the affairs of our alternative world."

"Good point!" barked Arjon. "See why this game is so great ... it allows us to see what is so good about our world, from the perspective of *what could have been*."

"So ... does the matrix show why such an outcome would have transpired?" asked Macrose.

"Yes!" Arjon could hardly contain his enthusiasm. "Because the alternative United Nations was created in an environment overshadowed by a global power struggle between the communists ... and those endorsing a popular form of government."

He added on a more serious note, "From my reading of articles from Hesta's matrix, people were living under the cloud of imminent attack from ballistic missiles during the 'Cold War.' The articles used terms such as 'nuclear deterrence,' 'mutually assured destruction,' and believe it or not, 'backyard fallout shelters.'"

The host allowed his stunned guests to digest his words. He'd had time to adjust to the frightening madness of the matrix, but from their expressions he was sure his guests thought he sounded slightly mad himself.

Despite their looks of incredulity, he continued buoyantly, "But behold! We live in a magically positive existence ... with empowered individuality, and the freedom and prosperity of a sane world. And it has all transpired because our predecessors stamped out humanity's oppressors!"

The bemused looks around the table awaited further

enlightenment.

"This game ... Hesta's matrix, it's all been an exercise in self-actualization. With all our wonderful technology, arts and inspiration, we still find it hard to realize just how much we have to be thankful for. The free world rolls along, humanity prevails over its own flaws and limitations, escapes the gravity of self-destruction, and heads out into the solar system."

Eya leant back and rolled her eyes at his expansive dialogue.

Arjon noticed her expression and looked around to check he wasn't boring his friends. They appeared to be in the same frivolous mood as before, so he kept postulating, "Onward we go ..." he raised his glass, "... not really knowing where we've been!"

Glasses clinked in salute, and Eya, feeling some relief that the preaching was over, added an addendum, "... or knowing what *could* have been."

∞

Death is nothing, but to live defeated and inglorious is to die daily.
Napoleon Bonaparte

Bialystok, Poland
April 23rd, 1946

Miles of marching GIs and slow-moving supply convoys streamed across the rain-soaked landscape. General Patton's staff car splashed through muddy potholes as it got waved through an intersection by an MP. With him in the rear compartment sat Colonel Corday, who leant out to the side so he could see the insignia on the soldiers' shoulder badges more clearly.

"This is the 144th Infantry ... they've just moved up from Brest."

Patton nodded. "This weather has only slowed down the

build-up ... it won't delay the operation."

"General, the enemy's resistance has been stiffening the closer we get to Russia, how do you see this panning out once we approach Moscow?"

"That's a good question Colonel," answered Patton, gazing out the window and far into the distance, as though he were casting his mind a thousand miles and six months into the future.

"Remember, this is a people who burned their own capital to deny it to Napoleon," he said ominously, "but communism is a sickness, a sickness that afflicts the weak minded. I liken it to the same deficiency in spirit that characterizes those who endure life beneath a monarchy. To appease their fate, they convince themselves it will provide them with security and stability ... but it ends up as slavery."

"Slavery?" asked Corday, sensing an opportunity to draw more of the pressurized inspiration contained within his commander's mind.

"Yes slavery. If a man can't aspire to the highest posts in his own country, can't speak his mind for fear of persecution ... then he is not free. His existence is nothing more than indentured servitude ... perpetually serving the state – or crown."

His blue eyes blazed at the thought of the war with the communists as a whole. He remembered the reports from the Eastern Front where hordes of poorly armed and untrained Soviet troops had been decimated by the Nazis. During Operation Barbarossa one German general had even described it as infanticide.

"*God-damn it!* Why are there so many ignorant sheep! Slaves to their state! They're like cattle to be slaughtered!"

His liberty-fueled passion abated, and in a more measured tone he added, "... and slaves to the tyrant at its head."

Corday was slightly taken aback at the outburst, "Yes sir, but aren't they also just patriots?"

"Hmmph ... yes ... perhaps, but they're patriots of evil."

The infantry were cheering as they passed, so the general leaned forward and tapped the driver on the back. The driver flipped a switch and the klaxons mounted on the front of the car blared loudly to return the greeting.

"Morale's high ..." said Patton, looking out at the waving soldiers and almost shouting to be heard. "How is it in your battalion?"

Corday smiled. "Sky-high." He also had to shout, "Another one of the benefits of playing on a team."

The wailing sirens stopped as they moved beyond the intersection.

Patton lowered his voice, "Are you saying your men are more motivated because they think war is a sport?"

"Not exactly sir ... but that kind of thinking would be a good outcome. I'd say high morale is more a result of the whole process we use in our game plans – the positive language, calling plays ... encouraging each other. The spirit of brotherhood we already have in the military is enhanced by the close teamwork and synergy that arises from working as a group of men who support each other, and depend on each other for everything."

Corday elaborated, "As you know, during the last war there could be problems with maintaining morale – even though we were winning. Like the military, the game of football is a system where all players work together to achieve a result. By superimposing the concept of a sport over that of fighting a war, we help the men handle their situation ... and take the fear of being in an armed conflict out of that situation. Fear is an obstacle to clarity of mind – to thinking clearly under pressure – so we remove that obstacle, and replace it with a will to win."

Patton listened thoughtfully, his mind working on ways to include Corday's game-plans into basic military training.

"Agreed. There are many facets of the sporting mindset that are not incompatible with the military," he said. "I can see how this approach could help the men ... and if you continue to have success, I'll work on getting it presented to the Chief of Staff."

A huge blast rent the air as a Red Army artillery shell exploded nearby. Patton, as usual didn't bat an eyelid. He looked off to the side of the road and watched the infantrymen who'd dived for cover picking themselves up from the mud. He sighed and added, "It might also help to reduce the amount of laundry they need to do."

∞

New York Times
April 24th, 1946

"KIEV FALLS!"

"The key city of Kiev in the Ukraine has been taken by Allied forces. The city was a major objective of the war's south-eastern theater, and the city's capitulation was the culmination of advances made by the Allies from the south. Those advances had been initiated by a series of landings by the Marine Corp and several Allied Armies in the Black Sea. Admiral Chester Nimitz has stated, "These victories have been made possible by the achievement of complete naval and air superiority in the region, and by the unmatched valor and determination of the men who comprise those forces."

April 24th, 1946
Supraśl River,
North-west of Bialystok, Poland

Patches of early morning sunlight, yellow-gold splashed on slick red-brown mud, sparked boyhood memories of eating breakfast in Kansas for Captain Deming.

Shucks, could I ever go for a bowl of cornflakes ...

He lifted his field glasses and scanned the opposite bank

of the quiet, swollen river. A wall of riotous greenery climbed up from the edge of the muddy bank, strangling the trees and making them appear as a forest of wild topiary. At the end of the trail below them, the slowly flowing water was disturbed where it bulged over a submerged crossing. Another one of the temporary bridges left behind by the retreating Soviets.

He ordered his driver to cut engines so he could listen for sounds coming out from the opposing wilderness.

Just echoing bird calls, and the agonizing silence of a waiting ambush.

They're always so goddamned quiet. Nothing but the sound of your own heart pounding in your ears … before you hear the crack of that first shot. That's if you live.

He spied the far trees again, then, scrutinized the bridge. The cold, rusty water simmered its way over the base of rocks and logs covered with gravel. The rutted tracks cutting their way down to the water's edge below, confirmed that Taskforce Barkley had passed this way during the night.

How far ahead they were now he wouldn't know until radio-silence was broken. Deming gave the signal to start engines. Dark birds took flight from the tree-tops on the far side. A murder of crows. An omen? Not for Deming – he saw it as something positive.

Good. If we startled them then there's little chance of there being anyone in there.

He waved the Hellcats behind him to go through, while his own troop remained in position to provide covering fire. After Veste Oberhaus, the battalion had been rested. It had given them time to train alongside some of the new tanks the 10th Armored Division had received. A task force of M26 Pershings and motorized infantry were the spearhead. Following Colonel Corday's tactical planning, the tank destroyers together with their half-tracks full of combat engineers were acting as a mobile defense, following up behind so they could protect the column's rear.

After the first three Hellcats had crossed, Deming knew that there were no Reds waiting for them on the other side. He waited for a half-dozen of the mixed M9s and M16 quad 50 caliber "meat choppers" to cross over, then got his driver to push their Hellcat back into the column.

Once across, the upland forest provided thick cover on both sides of the dirt trail. Fifty yards inside the trees they spotted the signs of Task Force Barkley's progress. Camouflage netting hanging from the branches, had been ripped apart by multiple explosions. The clinging vines and creepers were scorched to a shiny black-green, where a massive blast, probably from exploding ammunition, had destroyed an anti-tank emplacement.

The watchful eyes of the engineers peered into the gloom for any signs of life. The wreck of the dug-in howitzer, blackened and broken, looked like a distorted and macabre metal sculpture. Around the scattered bodies of the Red Army defenders, nothing stirred.

As the column left the scene of destruction behind, the crows returned to pick on the remains of their grisly morning meal.

Further down the trail, a burnt-out Pershing marked where the Soviets had deployed a second anti-tank gun to cover the first. The column swept past without sighting the source of the kill.

After another half-mile of nervous progress, and no further signs of resistance, Deming allowed himself to relax. He quickly shook off the moment as his battle experience forced him to stay frosty. They'd only been past a light defensive position … there must be more ahead. As if his instincts were serving him well, seconds later a huge thump shattered the peace.

The surrounding trees seemed to shudder from the shockwave. Helmeted heads lowered into their vehicles, and the Hellcats at the front of the column slowed cautiously, ready to take cover to the side of the track.

"Close up!" Deming called into his mike, and he saw the commanders of the lead tank destroyers drop down and close their hatches. The trees thinned to reveal pillars of smoke filling the sky.

They'd found the battle.

The tank destroyers pulled off the trail and formed up along the top of a low hill. Ten thousand acres of carnage confronted them. Hatches opened and the crews peered out in awe at the grim spectacle. Barbed wire and trenches stretched for miles. Flaming wrecks and smoldering bodies littered the battlefield. A current of warm air flowed off the plain carrying the smell of cordite, burning oil and death to the silent watchers.

Deming realized from the scale of the fighting that Task Force Barkley had joined up with Combat Command A and the right flank of the Division. He scanned ahead up to the horizon, but there was no way to tell where Task Force Barkley had gone amid the chaos.

He changed frequencies and the battle net crackled with urgent voices. ... *tank sighted!* ... *engaging machine gun post* ... *infantry anti-tank at two o'clock* ... *one hundred yards – fire!*

He switched back to battalion, "Coach, this is Quarterback ... over."

"Quarterback this is Coach, receiving you loud and clear ... over."

His radio operator handed him a piece of paper, "Coach ... message follows ..." and he proceeded to read the groups of letters which formed the encoded message.

"Oboe Fox Dog Victor Easy ... Able Charlie Easy Jig Zebra .... Mike Sugar William Uncle Victor ..."

Each five-letter group represented one letter, so reading the entire contents took over two minutes. When decoded by the receiving operator it explained that the platoon was in position and waiting for the go-ahead to join the battle.

Deming raised his field glasses and saw a line of tanks on fire in the distance. He exhaled with relief as he recognized their outlines as that of a group of T-34s. Their scorched turrets were turned side on with gun-barrels sagging, pointing impotently in the direction from which their attackers had killed them.

Minutes passed as they waited for Battalion to respond

to their request. The crew of the Hellcat stirred restlessly at their posts, with keen eyes switching from one likely course of approaching danger to another. The driver, Shelby, spat down onto the ground as though he were trying to get the taste of the air out his mouth.

"We gonna wait here all day while everyone else is kicking Ivan's butt?" he asked impatiently.

"We're waiting for Corday to put us in the game … just sit tight and enjoy the scenery," Deming replied laconically.

The commander's field glasses roamed hundreds of yards beyond the immediate area covered by the crew. With a dulled and cold dispassion, his view ranged past individual scenes of destruction. Hours or minutes before, men had fought, killed and died, but now there were only the tragic remains of their heroism and sacrifice.

Finally, battalion called back and advised them on Task Force Barkley's position. Deming clicked his mike in readiness to give to the order to move out, when a movement in his peripheral vision brought his senses to full alert. A dark green shape came sharply into focus, unfamiliar at first, but then Deming's mind made the association between pictures he'd seen at a briefing, and the real thing now approaching from a mile away – an IS3.

The latest model of Iosif Stalin, or IS tank, looked sleeker and more menacing that any of its predecessors. Deming's heart rate climbed as he realized the implications – it was trying to sneak along the right flank of Combat Command A. Its powerful 122mm gun could do a lot of damage if it got into CCA's rear.

His mind made an instant adjustment, "Target! Fifteen hundred … three o'clock!"

Deming assessed the situation. The IS3's gun would have a longer range than their own 90mm. They were just going to have to be better tankers to win this fight. He waved the other Hellcats to back off from the lip of the rise. Giving the enemy more targets would just make their aiming easier. He scrutinized the lay of the land around them. Away to their right, he noticed something a few hundred yards out, in the foreground between them and the approaching tank. Overgrown by the tall grass, and barely visible: Dragon's Teeth – a long line of angled concrete jaws, slanting inwards to allow a tracked vehicle to easily enter, but would snag them if they tried to reverse out.

Probably been there since the Germans were retreating here in '44, he thought as he continued to search for the best field of fire.

His years of experience soon told him where to put his tank destroyer and exploit the terrain, and find the right elevation and slope for optimum fire control.

"Shelby, put us a hundred yards to the right and further back down the slope … I want us in a defiladed position but still able to put rounds on him."

He also called up Lieutenant Ellery's M18 to take up the same position they were vacating.

That'll split their fire between the two of us.

The IS3 came steadily onwards. From their new position, the crew of the commander's Hellcat watched their prey, and waited.

Now only one thousand yards away, the Russian tank began to veer to its right, soon it would be directly between them and the rear of the Combat Command. Deming kept his glasses on it as he calmly explained to his platoon in his laconic mid-western drawl, "Now the rest of you boys stay back now … this one's ours."

The hum of the engine provided a reassuring insulation from the sound of the distant battle. Deming tapped the gunner on the shoulder and it was met with an affirmative thumbs-up.

"*Fire!*"

The 90mm armor-piercing round screamed across the plain at three thousand eight hundred feet per second. Even so, the moving tank was not an easy target.

To the Russian commander, looking out of the upturned

soup-bowl of his turret, the projectile narrowly missing his head sounded like the crack of doom.

He disappeared inside the tank, which seconds later turned toward the source of the incoming shell.

Deming watched intently, *Good ... he's going to charge us.*

"Drop back fifteen feet ..." he called to Shelby. "That's your rocking point!"

"Got it sir!" the driver said as he responded by kicking the Hellcat into gear and reversing sharply.

As they pulled back down the slope the air above them parted and slammed shut with a roar. The Russians' shot would have landed far behind them in the forest.

Ten seconds for them to reload ...

"Let's start rocking!" Deming called out.

It was the crew's term for the standard tactic of moving backward and forward from cover. Utilizing the Hellcat's hydramatic transmission, Shelby accelerated, then lurched to a halt fifteen feet up the slope.

Crrabooom!

The blast-wave from the gun's muzzle flattened the grass around the front of the M18.

Inside the IS3, the crew were rushing to reload. Wild-eyed looks pounced from one to another in the gloom, as a monumental clang on the hull burst cables and gauges loose from the turret's interior – a ricochet.

From atop the rise, Deming saw sparks fly off the tank, and a streak of light arc off into the sky. *Damn HEAT rounds ... bouncing off like AP.*

He called out, "Target hit!" as Shelby started backing off.

Corporal Spane, the gunner, looked at him questioningly.

Deming answered him. "Glanced off the left side of the turret ... keep 'em coming!"

"Should we aim for the tracks?" asked Spane, "Then kill him when he's dead in the water ..."

"No! I want to keep him coming ... try and put one on the gun mantle."

Another rock forward ... but this one was a well-timed feint to draw the Russians' fire. Shelby knew the enemy tank's reload time ... pull up with two or three seconds to spare, Ivan aims in ... about to fire ... Now! And he backs away just as the 122mm shot goes overhead.

Another rock forward, another round fired, another miss.

The IS3's commander smiled grimly as he spied the lightly-armored American tank destroyer through his periscope.

"*Hellcat* ..." he advised his crew dismissively, "... *nye vazh nee*."

No problem.

To the M18, the approaching tank presented a narrower, more difficult target now that is was coming head-on. Another round bounced off the triangular pike of its heavy frontal armor.

Deming was getting worried. The Russian was now within eight hundred yards. His thin-skinned Hellcat was becoming a bigger target to them the closer they came.

As another 122mm shell screamed past his ears, he furiously calculated the time remaining until the IS3 reached them. There was little doubt the enemy would have the advantage in a close fire-fight.

Spane asked, "Need to get Ellery's gun going? It'll split their fire ... might even panic them."

"Not yet ... I still want them to think there's only one of us up here."

Six hundred yards.

Deming closed his eyes. The darkness allowed him to think in isolation – to visualize the battle as it was unfolding with less distraction. In his mind, he looked down from above, seeing the Russian tank approaching, taking note of its speed, the remaining distance to their own position, and that of Lieutenant Ellery's Hellcat waiting below the slope one hundred yards to their left. It allowed him to confirm what he'd been planning to do all along.

"Load smoke!"

Spane looked up at his commander expectantly.

Five hundred yards.

Deming dropped down beside his gunner so he could explain precisely what they were going to do. His eyes fixed on to Spane's with a life and death look.

"Drop them fifty to seventy-five yards in front of him … no closer – he'll think we're covering our retreat."

Spane nodded, and adjusted his sights.

The Soviet commander watched through his scope, waiting for the American to come into view again. He knew his tank was sacrificing accuracy by firing on the move, but wanted to get as close as possible to negate the enemy's positional advantage.

The M18's turret came into view, and he saw a gray puff spout from its gun barrel. His mouth opened to give the fire order when the world outside suddenly went white.

"*Klaat!*" he cursed.

Blinded by the cloud of phosphorus, he gave the fire order anyway.

"*Zhaar!*"

Deming heard the round miss. One hit from the 122mm and they were dead. Making his sense of vulnerability worse, their Hellcat was now exposed because they'd ceased the rocking maneuver to maintain the rate of fire required to lay an effective smoke screen.

"Lieutenant Ellery move up!" he called over the radio.

Through their scopes the Russians saw the smoke clear momentarily, then another cascade of phosphorus blanketed their view. Traveling at twenty-five miles per hour, they would be at the base of the slope in under a minute.

More smoke rounds exploded in front of them.

The driver craned his neck as though being a few inches

closer would help him to see through the cloud of white.

He gasped, fumbling for the brake … but too late, as 45 tons of metallic momentum scraped tortuously and groaned to a dead stop.

With the nose of the stalled tank pointing uphill at an angle, the commander flew up through his hatch to see what had happened. He sank heavily back inside and yelled, "Dragon's Teeth! *Zaad! Zaad!*"

The order to back out was a futile one. The driver restarted the engine and tried desperately to reverse but the tracks were jammed between the reinforced concrete jaws.

The commander put his eye to the view scope, and cried with horror as he watched through the clearing smoke, a second tank destroyer two hundred yards away to their right. The IS3's exposed flank would now be a soft target. The Hellcat's barrel swinging directly toward him was the last thing he saw.

∞

Mojave City
2266 CE

Virtue is the unbroken center-line dividing right and wrong on the road to innocence.
Ji-Zhu Geist

The sun's rays lifted the scent of frangipani and cherry blossom into the morning air. Eya breathed in the fragrance, and knew that a pervasive sense of beauty would influence the day ahead.

As she tended her garden, Hesta's voice interrupted her communion with the flowers.

"A visitor has arrived, Arjon is responding."

Eya continued her caretaking, thinking how very strange it was to receive an unscheduled caller. In fact, she couldn't recall a previous instance when Hesta hadn't advised them beforehand after receiving notice from the network.

The transparent energy screen that formed the bower's front entrance dissolved as Arjon approached. The visitor was dressed in comfortable attire, but with a semi-formal cut. His collared tunic spoke of authority, but was made from skinteractive fabric which regulated body temperature. His composure was relaxed and peaceful.

"Good morning friend!" the man announced from across the threshold.

"Yes, it certainly is ..." Arjon replied.

"My name is Thiessen. I would like to impose briefly upon your time ... and hospitality."

Something about the man put Arjon at ease so he welcomed him inside.

Hesta procured a tray of refreshments and delivered them to Arjon's den via robo-server.

"May I first explain," Thiessen said almost apologetically, "that my visit is in no way intended to be disruptive."

Arjon nodded and smiled from behind his desk as he took a seat, and motioned Thiessen to do likewise.

"You see, we received confirmation from your bower's AI that this would be an appropriate time."

"Oh ... but there was no notice?"

"That's because there is a special protocol where we are concerned."

"We?"

"The Center of Truth."

The name struck Arjon like an electric shock.

"I ... I feel very ... honored!" he stammered. "But why?"

"Why come here – unannounced, to your tranquil home?" It was as though he were preparing Arjon for something disturbing.

"As you are aware we do not engage with the public," he said matter-of-factly. "We do not *receive* applications or grant audiences to prospective applicants ... or *anyone."*

Arjon sipped his tea, feeling more privileged the more that the man spoke.

"It is by necessity, as our purpose is to fulfill our function in a totally impartial and objective manner. Untainted by outside influences."

"That makes sense. No wonder so little is known about your organization."

"And so ... here we are ... and you're wondering why we have imposed ourselves upon your precious time."

Arjon put down his teacup and drew a breath in anticipation.

"It's because of your matrix."

Arjon thought for a moment, he wasn't going to bother to ask how Hesta's matrix had come to their attention, obviously it was either from the previous year's court case, or from the content that had required processing on the network somehow triggering the attention of the CoT's intelligence systems.

Seeing Arjon was unfazed, Thiessen continued. "While performing our task of verifying and securing the Truth, of ensuring the veracity of all things that encompass the Human Condition, we sometimes touch upon those less tangible elements of our existence. Having confirmed what we perceive to be the majority of truths about the known universe, we find ourselves focusing on those elusive facets; the ones we hope may guide us from a solely material version of the Truth, to a more *complete* version."

"So ... you speculate by working with simulations?"

"Yes. Imagination is a wonderful thing, don't you think?"

"Why sure, but aren't we talking about machines?"

"It's a moot point ... let's not get into a metaphysical discussion or I shall never leave you in peace. Whether organic or inorganic, it has no bearing on the reliability of the source. We take care of that."

Arjon wanted to further explore the concept of machines

using their imagination, but thought better of it, holding himself back from distracting his guest.

Thiessen continued on enthusiastically. "Let us say that the human race's knowledge has explained and catalogued all of the physical universe."

"Qwerty! That's a big statement ... then I guess there'll be no more Enlightenments?"

"Perhaps ... and that may be the ultimate point of perfection our society can attain."

Thiessen paused, a glint in his eye showed that he may know more than he was disclosing, "Or perhaps there will be more for us to discover beyond our physical existence. Our universe has a beginning ... and an end. Exactly what part humanity plays in that scenario, we believe, will not simply be explained by the physical workings of the universe."

"Yes! I see ..." Arjon said excitedly, "... as shown by the last Enlightenment – the existence of our soul. It's as though it has completed a kind of trinity; for three of the Pillars ... the Bureau of Sanity – the mind, the Spire of Evolution – the body, and now the CoT – the soul."

Thiessen nodded, "Very intuitive. And I suppose the Union of Nations could be seen as merely the executive arm of the other Pillars. Interesting."

He shrugged off the diversion from the point he was making. "But getting back to the Enlightenment, the fact that our soul can interact with this universe, this *dimension*," he allowed a moment for Arjon to digest what he was proposing, "means that our soul may be bound to it."

"Mmmm ..." Arjon mused for a moment, "So the mind occupies the brain, and there is some connection between our mind and our soul ... but that could be a restraint? That our souls too are ... contained within this universe?"

"We believe so ..."

"Bummer."

∞

Bialystok, Poland
May 2nd, 1946

"Cabbages … more damned cabbages," Sergeant Abe Cooper lamented to his crew, "… they're a mile wide and ten miles deep."

"C'mon, you know the Russkies love their borscht," the gunner Lance Corporal Keponee, replied.

"In fact, this region has been disputed by both the Russians and Germans," Cooper advised, "before being ceded to the Poles, so due to the high percentage of immigrant farmers the result will more than likely be Polish sauerkraut."

The magnified image of thousands of sprawling green acres disappeared as he put away his binoculars. He looked up at the sun high in the bright blue sky, feeling its heat emanating off the armor encircling his torso.

Dropping down into the turret of the Chaffee light tank, he said, "Okay you guys, it's going to be 127th Recon business as usual."

"You trying to break it to us gently?" asked Keponee, inspecting a round of the main gun's 75mm ammunition.

Cooper ignored him, realizing the effects of the highly-motivating pep talk given by Colonel Corday that morning would have worn off of his crew by now, "The good news is there's a solid looking dirt track running downhill through the valley."

"And?" Keponee enquired as he replaced the round back in its rack and picked out the next in line.

"The bad news is there could be anything in the forests on either side."

The driver, Greene, who had been peering out of his front hatch, lowered into his seat and faced his commander. "Like you said, it's business as usual."

"Man, you should be honored that Uncle Sam chose *us*, this insignificant bunch of highly-trained nobodies, to perform this critical reconnaissance mission."

"I *am* honored … so much that my chest puffed out and all my medals popped off onto the floor of this fine little tank."

"Well then, we'll just have to go and earn you some more, won't we?"

Keponee grinned as he checked the firing controls and then the sights on the 75mm. He held the Company record for one-shot kills, although due to the gun's limited effectiveness against heavy armor, those kills were all anti-tank guns or thin-skinned transport. To downsize the gun for mounting in the M24's turret, it had been modified with a thinner barrel and a lighter recoil mechanism than the original anti-shipping version than the one equipped on the B-25 Mitchell bomber.

It irked the gun-aimer whenever he thought of such a precisely engineered weapon being used in such a haphazard way. Rounds being blasted all over the ocean from an aircraft moving at three hundred miles per hour. In contrast, he treated his craft as if he were a sniper with a very large rifle. A French-Canadian who had moved to the United States before the war, he thought of himself as a painter, his brush-strokes producing a Renaissance masterpiece, banging away at ships produced a kind of abstract art, where the paint had been thrown randomly at the canvas.

Cooper took a final scan around with his field-glasses, stifling the rising fear that stemmed from thoughts of an ambush. It was times like these that he thought of his brother, a marine who'd served in the Pacific. He'd been injured during the Black Sea landings a month ago, losing his pitching arm.

No more fast-balls on the weekend for you brother.

With renewed resolve, he reached down to the spot on the outside of the turret where the tank's nickname, *"Three-Z,"* was painted, giving the armor a pat for good luck. He pulled closed the top hatch. Inside the dimly lit turret the crew were completing their halt checks prior to resuming the mission.

"Report!" Cooper barked.

"Gunner ready!"

"Wait ..." Greene said, tapping the fuel indicator dial which promptly moved from zero to its correct reading, "Driver Ready!"

"Bog ready!"

"Loader ready!"

Satisfied they were prepared to roll out, he gave his final instructions. "Greene, I want everything out of this baby as soon as we roll," he told the driver.

Greene put his eye to his periscope, tracing a path forward along the track as it wound down the valley.

"Once the downhill section levels off, start zig-zagging ... but keep in mind we may need to do an about-turn – so make sure you leave enough room for that."

"Flat out, then start dancing ... you got it."

"Hap," Cooper said to the bow gunner, or Bog, "keep the .30 cal on the forest. Fire at anything that moves."

The sound of the machine gun being cocked was the only confirmation received from the front gunner.

"And short bursts only! That ammo's so expensive a box is worth more than a week's pay. Okay – let's move out!"

The twin Cadillac engines growled as Greene gave the M24 some revs. The ear flaps on the crew's leather helmets dampened the sound of the tracks rolling over the drive cogs as the Chaffee headed down the incline into the valley.

Given full throttle, Three-Z took off like a thoroughbred out of the starting gates. At forty miles per hour, Greene eased off slightly and let gravity do some of the work to take them the rest of the way down the pot-holed dirt track to the valley floor.

Cooper swiveled his periscope around, searching for signs

of the enemy in the wooded slopes on either side. It wasn't a matter of *if* they were there ... just when they were found. Earlier sightings from foot patrols through the forest had confirmed the Reds were active in this valley. Determining exactly where, and whether they had prepared defensive positions, was the scout tank's job.

Forty-four miles per hour.

Cooper thought he felt the tank leave the ground momentarily.

"Er ... Greene ..."

"Whoo-hoo ... we're air recon!" called the driver, then in a less enthusiastic voice said "... I know ... I know ... just let me get her to forty-five!"

"*Greene!*"

Cooper sensed an immediate deceleration. Thirty seconds later they leveled off onto flat ground.

"Eyes on those trees!"

The tank slowed and Greene began to deftly manipulate the controls. They left the firmly packed surface of the road and moved onto the cultivated field to their left. The furrowed soil of the rows of young cabbages slowed them even further.

The driver put them into a curving arc so that they wouldn't present as predictable a target. It was all they could do.

As a scout in the recon platoon they simply had to go out and locate any hostiles. The speed of the Allied advance sometimes demanded risky and unsafe tactics. In this case, the division needed to pass through this valley ... today.

Completing their first semi-circular sweep, they crossed over the road to the fields on the other side. Cooper thought of the irony of their situation. If there was an ambush waiting up in the forest, they could only succeed in their mission if they sprang it.

Not a job for the faint-hearted.

If the Reds let them through to see if anything was coming along behind, then the scout tank would have failed.

Cooper yelled over his mic, "*Hap! Time to go to work!*"

The Bog opened up with the .30 cal.

As the piston-hammer beat of the machine-gun rang in their ears, the crew could see the rounds streaming out toward the woods.

Incendiaries.

As Greene swung them to within two hundred yards of the tree-line, rounds that found a solid enough surface such as dry bark or branches, ignited on impact. The zirconium sponge inside the tips exploded at five thousand degrees.

Instant wild-fire.

The Chaffee wheeled away from the string of growing fires, bumped over the track and then started more fires on the other side. Cooper knew that as they became more intense, even well-entrenched troops wouldn't stick around in the face of an advancing wall of flames.

More sweeps, and a dozen fires were soon blazing behind them.

Cooper was getting anxious, still no reaction. Maybe the Reds had already pulled back. *Suits me, nothing like an easy day's work* ... and he started thinking of how to make the best use of the upcoming weekend pass.

Claaaang!

It sounded like a sledgehammer had struck the turret. A ricochet.

"Where's it from?" called Cooper.

"Got it ..." Hap had seen the muzzle-flash from just off to one side from where he was aiming his next spray from the .30 cal.

He instantly changed aim. "Laying fire on target!"

Bright orange rounds squirted into the woods in a continuous stream.

I don't care if that's a month's pay ...

Greene kept them running straight at the ambush, but backed off the speed to help out the gunners.

From either side of where Hap's rounds were going, automatic weapons fire was coming back at them. The invisible rain of thudding steel hammered away at the tank's inch-thick armor in the background, but the crew were too focused on killing the ambush for it to register.

Keponee never took his eye off the target area. He'd held his fire, waiting for a couple of seconds of level ground, before finally pulling the trigger.

From only one hundred yards, the 75mm high explosive shell hit something, because sparks burst out a fraction of a second before a fireball erupted skywards among the trees.

"Hit!" he shouted, but the others had seen the flash anyway.

Hap stopped firing for a second, checking his aim, then resumed as soon as he saw blinking muzzle flashes from entrenched infantry.

On the receiving end, the Soviet soldiers had to quickly adjust their range as the approaching American tank had closed underneath their sights.

One soldier, in frustration, stood up in his trench to improve his aim. An incendiary bullet struck his forehead square on. It penetrated his skull before igniting, instantly incinerating his brain. Contained within his steel helmet, the jets of flame had nowhere else to go but to vent out through his eye sockets and mouth. A commie jack-o-lantern.

"*Get us out of here!*" Cooper yelled, as he saw two puffs of smoke appearing from the woods several hundred yards ahead. More anti-tank guns.

Explosions rocked the Chaffee from side to side as they charged across the field.

"*C'mon, c'mon* … they're getting the range … fire smoke!"

"Firing smoke!" Keponee responded, as the main gun was being loaded. He stabbed at a button on a control box and an 80mm mortar mounted on the side of the turret coughed out a bomb. It landed behind them, spouting white phosphorus into the air. The cloud provided precious seconds of cover, as they completed their turn and got back on to the dirt track.

Greene pushed the M24 to its maximum speed as the enemy anti-tank guns peppered their wake with explosions. Cooper hated showing the enemy the Chaffee's tail, where its armor was weakest. They rotated the turret as they sped off, firing more phosphorus from the main gun.

Once out of range, and leaving behind a spate of forest fires along with a very angry regiment of Russians, the crew let out a collective sigh of relief. Time resumed its normal passage, slowing down from the fire-fight where every minute had been compressed into fractions of a second, and back to a heartbeat of normality.

"Well, we did it!" Cooper said, complimenting his crew.

"And lived to tell about it … *dieu merci!*" added Keponee.

Greene patted Three-Z on the inside of her hull, "Man, she lived up to her name again, Zpeed, Zwerves and Zmoke – she's got 'em all."

They didn't need to call in their discovery over the radio. An artillery observation post at the top of the valley had already called it in. By the time the Chaffee was safely back at the head of the trail, a squadron of Douglas A26 Invaders were flying in at low altitude. They had a very clear indicator of their target – the furthermost area of woods on fire.

The hatches on the light tank popped open and Cooper's crew watched as the first medium bomber strafed the edge of the woods with its multiple 20mm-nose cannon.

Trees splintered and shattered in a maelstrom of shredded greenery. Cooper would have felt sympathy for those scrambling for cover in the burning forest, but years of war had hardened him from such emotions. His dispassionate eyes merely reflected the unfolding carnage. The Invader finished its run by dropping six thousand pounds of bombs.

The Russians' trenches provided no shelter. Huge columns of fire lifted flaming fir and pine trees into the air. The tons of fiery timber were tossed around as though weightless, then tumbled back to earth to feed the growing firestorm.

Cooper's satisfaction intensified as the bonfire grew. A second bomber went in, then a third. A holocaust of cannon-fire and bombs ensued as plane after plane unloaded, until a two-mile stretch of valley had become a cauldron from which no life would emerge.

Assholes.

That was for you brother.

"Alright, show's over, let's get out of here."

∞

History teaches us with unmistakable emphasis that appeasement begets new and bloodier wars.
Douglas MacArthur

"Where are we?" Arjon asked Thiessen, shivering at the BlindFold-induced cold.

"Chosin Reservoir ... North Korea."

He looked around him with a bleak indifference that blended well with the frozen rock of the surrounding mountainside.

Arjon knew that Korea was a country in Southeast Asia, but he hadn't heard a reference to "North" before.

An icy wind penetrated past his shivering skin and gripped his bones.

"W ... why are we here?" he chattered through clenched teeth.

"To show you what lies beyond your AI's original simulation. We needed to see a bigger picture. One that confirms the state that the Earth would be in with an ineffective Union of Nations."

A distant thunder ebbed through the blustering wind.

Arjon wondered at Thiessen, standing, looking over the edge of a precipice in the direction of the thunder, and seemingly oblivious to the conditions. Although he was dressed in the

Skinteractive tunic, it didn't seem as though his insulation stemmed from anything physical. It was more that his mind was engrossed in a great purpose which removed his environment to an insignificant background.

The thunder grew in intensity, until the percussion could be felt through the thin air. Arjon realized it wasn't being caused by storm clouds, but cannon fire.

A staccato burst of machine-gun fire followed, then a cacophony of small arms, explosions and yelling.

The ground beneath Arjon's feet shuddered with the trembling quake of rock being blasted nearby. He had to check himself mentally, almost being consumed by his sensory integration with the BlindFold. The cold was forgotten as he joined Thiessen at the edge of their vantage point, and watched with horror as on the snow covered slopes below, a sparse line of United Nations troops fired desperately into an approaching swarm of attacking soldiers. The advancing horde were wearing distinctive fur caps and dull khaki quilted jackets.

Chinese.

"What does this all mean?" Arjon asked pleadingly. "Those men are hopelessly outnumbered ..."

"We have analyzed multiple iterations of this simulation ... trying to determine all of the contributing factors that have led to this ... situation."

Arjon listened with only half of his attention, most of which remained riveted to the tragedy unfolding below.

Hundreds of Chinese communists were being cut down, but thousands more kept coming. As the smoke and explosions from grenades, artillery and gunfire obscured the height of the battle, the viewers could only see the lines of UN soldiers filtering away from the carnage as they executed a fighting withdrawal.

"So you see," Thiessen spat with disgust, "... this is the result of yet another example of the lack of commitment and pusillanimity shown by the world leaders of this alternate history."

The simulation closed.

Thiessen explained. "Those men were fighting for the *United Nations* – against an invasion of the South by the North Koreans. The North Koreans had been beaten – driven back to the Chinese border ... then the Chinese attacked."

With a pained expression, he continued, "The rules of engagement imposed upon the commander of the UN forces, General Douglas MacArthur, were that he could not contain the attacking Chinese with airstrikes against their airfields in China, or their lines of supply coming across the border. Effectively, he was tasked with fighting a war with one hand tied behind his back."

Arjon removed his BlindFold, exhausted from the chilling reality of both the atrocious conditions, and the shock of witnessing the battle.

"That doesn't sound very reasonable? Why? Who?"

"MacArthur labeled those in power as 'appeasers.' It appears there was considerable fear of a more widespread conflict with the communists."

"It's hard to believe ... another horrible war."

He thought of his life now, in a world that had known only peace for three centuries, and then remembered how human history before that had been stained by the barbarity of violence.

"Yes, it appears that the tragedy of human history continues unabated in this alternative world, and that in their ignorance, they have failed to overcome the instinctive savagery that is characteristic of our primitive origins," Thiessen advised sadly.

"Our investigations have uncovered the same disturbing trend ... that of perpetual conflict scarring this alter-humanity."

Reclining within the comfort of the bower, Arjon put his head in his hands and thought deeply.

A robo-serve brought cups of a refreshing nectar, and then withdrew silently.

"So ..." Arjon finally said after recovering some of his composure, "when comparing this to our own history, it seems that the influence of a determined General, and those of similar visionary minds, have helped us to avert this onerous fate?"

"So it would seem."

"But that notion would challenge the accepted ideology that our peaceful utopian society was founded on the principles espoused by the teachings of the great philosophers and spiritual figures from our past – such as the Dalai Al Pakha, Burrudha and Ji-zhu Geist?"

"Principles of non-violence and dare I say it ... pacifism?"

"There will no doubt be an outcry if we do not present these findings extremely carefully."

"Carefully? Qwerty! There hasn't been a war in three centuries!" Arjon cried, unable to keep his voice down. "There isn't a standing army on the planet! If we start proclaiming the warriors of our past as the ones upon which whose deeds the foundations of our society have been built, it could have catastrophic consequences."

"Perhaps," Thiessen conceded. "But the *truth* must be known!"

He made the statement as though it were a doctrine by which his life was given purpose.

Arjon got up and paced around his den like a caged animal. All his life he, as with everyone he'd ever known, had accepted that their utopian society had prevailed by way of peaceful determination. A natural evolutionary process where humanity as a whole had shunned violent confrontation, and the evil influences in humans had magically faded away to allow the good to emerge uncontested and victorious.

That was who they were.

That was who Ji-Zhu Geist and the other idealists were.

Humanity held on to those examples, those role models, as though they were a part of themselves. Now the warriors of the past were to be introduced to the halls of honor.

"Why bring this to light?" Arjon asked, seeing how disruptive the discovery could be. "Why risk perfection ... at the expense of simply not disclosing some perspectives of our past – speculative ones at that?"

Thiessen stood up, his eyes flashing with indignation, "Our society and hence, our common psyche – the so-called 'human condition,' *depends* on it!"

He strode to the open doorway, looking out and seeing Eya tending her garden across the way.

"If we fear the truth, we will never be truly free ... or enlightened."

He looked back at Arjon, "We have risen above the darkness of human history, the insanities of tyranny and war, and the futility of pointless decadence ... but we must continue to do so with courage, and not appease our fears."

With that he left, and as he walked across the open expanses of the center of the bower to exit, Eya looked up from her gardening. As she wondered what the stranger's visit was about, she watched Arjon leave his den and approach, a troubled expression on his face.

"Who was that?"

Arjon saw the front energy screen reforming to a close, then sighed, "Someone I'm sure we will be seeing again."

"Oh ... why?"

"I'm not certain, but I think he may need my help with an Enlightenment."

∞

May 11ᵗʰ, 1946
North-East of Bialystok, Poland

The afternoon sun painted a landscape bathed in gold. The light was a temporary reprieve before the coming darkness. It gave a vitality, an air of renewal to a blasted and dead vista that only a few days before had been a lush woodland studded with birch and oak.

Four blackened and crumbling walls were all that remained of a farmhouse standing alone amidst the broken countryside. A steady influx of armored vehicles to its vicinity signified its status as the forward command post of the 558th Tank Destroyer Battalion.

Inside, a briefing was under way for the following day's advance. Colonel Corday, although haggard and sleep-deprived from three months of continuous warfare, still exuded the energy of a football coach revving up his players before a game.

The operation to reduce the defenses around Krynki had been an unrelenting grind for the past ten days. The colonel looked across the map table at his team of officers. Their five-o'clock shadows and sweat-stained shirts belied the enthusiasm of a group ready to exert all of their efforts into making sure the battalion was given every chance for success.

The Allied push across Poland had been swift but costly. Up until now, the bulk of the battalion's planning had been to coordinate the use of their units with those of the 10th Armored Division, with tank destroyers being used to support the forward thrust of the main armor. In trademark Patton style, the 3rd Army's advance had been relentless, not allowing the Red Army any time to consolidate. But Poland had been mostly flat, easily traversed terrain, ideal for fast moving armored divisions with complete air superiority above them.

As a result, the Soviets had withdrawn while building up fortifications where it mattered most to them – here, on the border of their homeland.

"The division has finally weakened the Reds' outer positions here ... and here."

Corday pointed to either side of a salient, where a bulge was forming in the thick red line marked on the map.

"Tomorrow morning the GHQ tank battalion will exploit the weakness on the south-western flank and is expected to break through." He turned to the group of officers with a shrewd look, "But that doesn't mean it'll be easy going. The weakness in the Soviet line just means they haven't rushed up their reserves to fill it. They are probably doing this deliberately, with the expectation that we will attack there." His brow furrowed, "That means they have more in store for us as we push deeper into their defenses."

A low murmur among the officers died down as Captain Peters asked a question intended to quieten his colleagues' concern. "What'll the preliminaries be?"

"Heavy aerial bombardment, as well as an artillery barrage. Two additional artillery regiments have been moved up to support the offensive."

"Whew ..." whistled Peters. "Another hundred and twenty big guns, plus the indirect firepower from three hundred tanks ... should be better than fourth of July fireworks."

"Strategic command wants this one to get the commies' attention. The other divisions on either side will be attacking, but mainly to support the 10th Armored's flank."

The officers huddled closer as Lieutenant Clay laid several large black and white photographs down on the map, "Our recon flights today have given us a good picture of what we'll be up against. Apart from the miles of trench systems we've been encountering, there are heavier fortifications extending for miles inland from the front."

"That area doesn't look any heavier defended than that in front of it," Captain Peters observed.

"No ... because the earthworks are of a type we've never seen, more widely dispersed, and on a massive scale."

Clay produced another photo, this one taken by a recon fighter from a much lower altitude, "This close-up shows how they've camouflaged a road with netting ... this leads for miles back to the rear. And here ... see these tank tracks disappearing into what appears to be a grass covered hillside? Intelligence provided by the local partisans has been describing underground excavations with disguised entrances ... tank parks invisible from the air."

"How much armor have the Russkies got left? They've got no airforce ..." asked one of the Company commanders.

"That's why our recon flights can get in to do such a thorough job ... and there's only minimal AA spread out thinly over such a large area," Clay answered, "but the Reds' tank factories have been producing with only minor interruption. Every time our bombers hit them they have the production lines repaired in a matter of days ... we can expect their tank armies to be at near full-strength."

"Apart from the tank parks, what else can we expect?" asked Captain Peters.

"Everything except the trench systems are either underground or concealed under forests or camo nets ... dug-in tanks and anti-tank weapons, and plenty of artillery."

Corday could see the heavy pressure of pessimism weighing on the minds of his officers. Serious expressions, deep in concentration trying to foresee how their individual units were going to prevail in the upcoming battle. The Russian defenses were going to be a formidable obstacle to overcome. The Colonel took a deep breath, sensing that his next words were going to be crucial in allaying their fears. He needed to instill confidence in them to do their duty, and then through them, on to the men under their respective commands.

"Boys, this is what we're here for."

All eyes looked up and met his.

"This is going to be the big one – we win here and the road's wide open to Moscow. You men know what we've done before ... what this Army has done before ... how General Patton has led us over a thousand miles of heavily defended enemy territory, and we've rolled right through them."

His eyes blazed, penetrating the negativity in the room like a tornado – the pessimism vanished in the gale, replaced by an impregnable resolve.

"This is going to have the same victorious outcome. It's just a matter of when."

"Once the Division's armor has broken through, we will not be following up in the same way we have in the past … this time we will have a completely different purpose."

He indicated to the map, running a finger along the left prong of the upturned horseshoe-shaped bulge in the line. "We will be skirting around the edge of the red line, following the GHQ armor, which will push inwards once they reach this point here …"

His finger stabbed at the top of the horseshoe, where it bent inward, and the gap between the two prongs was at its narrowest.

"Naturally the overall objective will be for the 3rd Army divisions to advance across the top of the salient, cutting off and encircling the Red Army units within it."

His finger traced across to the top of the right prong.

"Regardless of the strategic outcome, our role will be to divert from behind the GHQ armor, and instead of our usual role of providing support in case of a counter-attack, we will swing up toward Kuźnica, along this road, and use the more open terrain to conduct harassment operations against any red armor coming in to support Krynki. Captain Deming will be commanding three companies of Hellcats in addition to his own unit, and directing them once through the breach."

He looked up at his officers, smiling with satisfaction in the face of their unwavering attention. "We will be utilizing the M18's major asset – its speed."

There were no looks of surprise around the table at hearing all of this – they'd been training for it.

"Our tank destroyers following up the light tanks of the 127th

Recon Company will be accompanied by units of the British LRDG and French Foreign Legion."

There were nods and looks of appreciation among the officers. Those allied units were highly mobile, and had been training with the battalion in Poland. Both the Long Range Desert Group and the Legionnaires were units whose skills had been forged in the vast expanses of North Africa. Their ability to remain concealed, and use of hit and run tactics in wide open spaces, were going to be invaluable on the open steppe.

"This task force will only follow the Kuźnica road for two miles, then disperse to either side – using mobility to maximize our disruption of the enemy rear."

"Sir?" asked another of the Company commanders. "Is that section of the road going to be clear?"

"As clear as we can make it. In addition to being a concentrated target of the preliminary barrage and air-strikes, there will be coordinated attacks and sabotage on enemy facilities by partisans along the route, and the M24s of the recon company will be calling in squadrons of fighter bombers specially assigned for this operation, waiting on standby overhead."

"What do we know about the partisans?"

"As you know, the town of Krynki had a large population of Jewish citizens who were the victims of genocide by the Nazis. Now, together with elements of the Polish underground, some of those original inhabitants have returned to this area and are active against the Soviet presence. Due to the Russians' history of atrocities against the Jews, the locals have as much contempt for them as they do for the Nazis."

The rest of the briefing's detail was unimportant, the battalion was primed and ready. Once in the enemy rear, they were going to hit the Reds hard, and then fade away before the slower Soviet armor could retaliate.

Dawn the following day brought rain. Clearing showers and a gray sky, but it wouldn't be enough to slow down the attack. Nor would it be enough to keep the Allied air power from the skies.

At 0400, as the Hellcat crews finished their pre-operation checks, they paused to watch the waves of heavy bombers, B17s and B29 Superfortresses, passing high overhead. Minutes later, flying much faster and at a lower altitude, hundreds of medium bombers, mostly Liberators and B26 Marauders, winged their way toward Red Army ground targets.

An umbrella of death – the Allied troops on the ground drew strength from the awe-inspiring sight.

The faster low-level bombers would be over their targets first, lighting them up with incendiaries for the heavy bombers following behind, and then continuing out of the danger zone before the rain of hell came down from above.

Fifteen minutes later, the very earth shook as the Allied artillery was unleashed on the Soviet positions.

Massed along a twenty-mile front, dozens of battalions of 155mm M1 Long Toms and M12 King Kongs, as well as 203mm M43s, saturated the Red Army lines with high explosive.

At 0430, the 558th Tank Destroyer battalion moved out from their rally point to follow up the GHQ armor. Captain Deming's M18 took point as they motored along a rough track in single file. Behind them trailed a long column of slower moving half-tracks carrying infantry and combat engineers with anti-tank guns. These were to follow up and hold key positions along the road to prevent any Red Army forces from getting in behind the fast-moving main advance.

Deming kept an eye on the sky for any black clouds, but if anything, the patchy sunlight was getting brighter. Movement from behind caught his attention. The troop of scout tanks was closing up and would soon pass them.

Deming waved and called the lead Chaffee on the radio.

"Wideout Leader, this is Quarterback ... over."

"Quarterback this is Wideout Leader ... reading you loud and clear – over."

As the Chaffee fell in beside the Hellcat and matched speed, Deming recognized Abe Cooper from their time in training at Camp Hood.

"Morning Sergeant ... you missed our breakfast invitation, but we're planning a barbecue at lunchtime in Krynki. You're welcome to join us."

Cooper tipped his helmet and replied, "We'll take you up on that Captain ... mind if we go on ahead and pick out a nice shady spot?"

"Be our guest, but I don't think the Reds will have left many trees."

He spotted several scarred gouges from ricochets on the Chaffee's turret. One larger one even allowed a snip of daylight to show through.

"You should get Ordnance to fix those holes ... before your luck runs out of 'em."

"Luck?" laughed Cooper, "We don't need any of that ... just speed, swerves ... and smoke."

Across the scratchy radio link, Deming was sure he heard him say *"Zpeed, Zwerves and Zmoke."*

The scouts resumed their faster pace, and cruised past the column. Up and over the rolling terrain, they were soon lost from sight.

∞

Mojave City
2266 CE

The Great Hall resonated with the excited hum of an impending announcement. The Orator raised his hand in a gesture of greeting, and the hum subsided. In another ten thousand Halls around the planet, half of the Earth's population was also watching.

"People of the Free World ..." he began, "The Center of Truth has ratified a new Enlightenment."

The audience waited in excited anticipation. "However ..." he faltered, his usually implacable confidence dented by a look of uncertainty, "... due to unprecedented circumstances, the Protectorate must delegate this presentation to another ... entity."

Bewildered looks in the crowd threatened to burst into vocal protest. This had never occurred in the CoT's two centuries of existence.

The Orator continued, "A representative from an independent legal firm, Decatur and Associates, will be presenting the findings."

A gasp reverberated through the Halls, an unheard-of agency presenting an Enlightenment? What was going on?

The Center of Truth, Utopia's cradle of stability, was being rocked.

"This is to ensure that ..." the Orator advised with some indignation, "... there will be no conflict of interest caused by the nature of the truths about to be disclosed."

What was happening? The bedrock of civilization ... a conflict? From where? The other Pillars?

The Orator left the podium leaving more questions than answers.

Moments later, billions of eyes watched intently as a solitary figure entered the stage.

Arjon was clearly overwhelmed. His mind was reeling at the enormity of the situation, and with trepidation at what he was about to say.

∞

Krynki Salient,
May 12th, 1946
0730 HRS

Sargent Cooper had wondered what it may have been like on the surface of the moon. He was pretty sure if you just added a lot of scrap metal then this would be it. The previous weeks of fighting had produced an ashen, cratered emptiness, littered with wreckage and devoid of life.

As the group of scout tanks cruised north-east at thirty miles per hour, Cooper scanned the horizon searching for the tail of the 10th Armored Division columns. For miles ahead, the division would be skirting around the western edge of the Krynki salient, probing for weak spots.

Three-Z was riding along smoothly, following in the compacted earth of the dozens of tracks made by the heavy tanks of one of the Division's armored columns. The occasional burned-out bunker or dug-in Red Army tank with only its wrecked turret visible above ground, showed where the column had been delayed before moving on again.

Before long, the sounds of fresh conflict reached their ears. As they approached the top of a rise, Cooper's lead tank slowed to a crawl, and the platoon commander motioned with his arm for the other three Chaffees to do likewise.

As scouts, Cooper and his crew were more used to prowling around solo searching for the enemy ahead of the Division. Identifying targets was fairly straightforward – you could shoot first because you were the only friendlies out there. He had a feeling today was not going to be a normal day's work.

"Keponee easy on that trigger ... wait until I give the order before firing on any bogeys. Things may get more confusing than we're used to."

Nearing the top of the incline, Cooper watched from the commander's hatch as the blue sky slowly met the other side of the slope.

Armageddon was in full-swing. The 10th Armored's heavy tanks, T30 Mammoths and T32 Grizzlies, supported by infantry from the 87th and 26th Infantry Divisions, were assaulting across a wide front. The Chaffees idled for several minutes while for several minutes, Cooper used his field glasses to try to determine how the battle was going. He could see two clear lines of advance where the fighting was the most intense. These would be Combat Commands A and B, he thought. One of these, it was hoped, would turn into a breach in the Russian line, allowing the Chaffees to follow through as planned.

He spotted a T95 Leatherjacket not far from their position, well behind the most forward American units. Its role was to tackle any tougher obstacles left behind by the faster moving heavies. The T95 fired a round from its extra-long barrel, into a bunker complex one hundred yards to its front. It exploded on the outside of the eight-foot thick concrete of the bunker, sending a cloud of gray powder and smoke into the air. From inside the bunker, an anti-tank gun returned fire. Cooper saw its shell strike the tank square-on. There was no explosion as the armor-piercing shell impacted the tank's 11 inches of frontal armor, which was too thick for the AT round to penetrate.

The Leatherjacket kept rolling as though it had just received no more than a slap in the face. At ninety yards, the Reds switched to HE and fired again. Same result, but this time there was some flame and smoke from the explosion.

At eighty yards, the T95 fired. Its 155mm High-explosive Squash-head, or HESH round slammed straight into the edge of the firing slit. Cooper had heard about the new HESH shells, and knew the effect they would be having inside the fortification. The plastic explosive in the shell's nose flattened on impact. When it detonated, the shock-wave resonated through the solid concrete, and resulted in a deadly shower of fragments, or spall, blasting the anti-tank gunners within.

Infantry supporting the Leatherjacket finished the job. A satchel charge was thrown through the opening, which exploded with a jet of flame venting from the recently widened firing slit. Multiple detonations followed as the ammunition inside went up.

Position reduced.

The Chaffees shut down their engines at their halt point as the battle slowly progressed. The crews got out for a stretch, but Cooper and his radioman stayed on post so they wouldn't miss the expected message from HQ for them to proceed. The commander leant his torso out over the flat top of the turret, focusing his glasses intently on one of the lines of advance.

Hurry up and wait ...

Combat Command B was forcing a gap in the Red lines a mile to the north, and about a mile to the west of Combat Command A, which appeared to be getting bogged down in a dense system of minefields and trenches.

He could see where one of CCA's tanks had been destroyed after its tracks had been blown off by a mine, making it an easy target for the enemy anti-tank guns. Combat engineers had then moved in and cleared a path so that the tanks behind could continue on. More difficult to make out at that range was the close-quarter combat raging around the rows of trenches. US infantry would occupy a trench, then have to fight savagely around every corner against the desperate Russians, trying to hold the last line of defense before the war entered their homeland.

Just before midday, Cooper got a radio message to advance. CCB had made its way through to the Kuźnica road. Cooper waved his troop forward. The four light tanks now had orders to reach the head of CCB on the left flank of the Division's advance. On the map, this would be the top of the left prong of the horseshoe. Once they reached the road, they were to spread out and find the enemy.

As they rolled, a flight of fighter bombers roared low overhead, called in to hit the Russians retreating ahead of CCB.

Go get 'em boys, thought Cooper, *don't let any of the sons of bitches get away ... else we'll just have to beat 'em again tomorrow.*

Cooper's platoon reached the Kuźnica road in the early afternoon. Combat Command B had halted, and the infantry were finishing up clearing out a roadblock. As the Chaffees turned onto the road and headed north, they watched as behind them a T32 Grizzly fired its gun into a bunker and gutted it. From one side of the bunker, a group of Russian infantry jumped out of their trench and rushed the tank. Several were cut down, but one made it close enough to throw an anti-tank grenade onto the T32's engine compartment just behind the turret. Shouting a curse, he then threw himself onto the ground beside the tank. The grenade's shaped charge detonated on impact. The explosion blew up the engine and fuel tank, sending out jets of flame from around the base of the Grizzly's turret. Two of the crew scrambled out from the front hatches engulfed in flames. Burning oil showered down onto the Russian soldier. His screams of agony fell on dispassionate ears as he writhed around and roasted.

With the assurance from air recon that the road ahead was clear, Cooper's troop sped onwards. The commander reflected how scenes like the one they had just witnessed no longer affected him. In the war against the Nazis the GIs weren't aware of the full measure of what they were fighting for until it was almost over, and the horrors of the Holocaust were made public.

The Allied soldiers in this campaign against the communists were different. The information war of the preceding year had seen to that. They knew what their enemy was capable of, and had become killers without question. As far as they were concerned, the communists were no different to the Nazis – guilty of indiscriminate extermination of people, albeit for the cause of collectivism, and for the perpetuation of Party ideology.

Why don't we just drop a fucking A-bomb on them? he thought.

Cooper was from a small town in Arkansas. To him, the US had fought the war to get back at the Japs for Pearl Harbor.

If it was good enough for them, what's the difference here?

He also knew the political view was different. Although the

fledgling Union of Nations feared Soviet expansionism, they still weren't comfortable with the idea of a conflict being settled by a weapon of mass destruction.

Too much collateral damage ... and so here we are.

The booming sound of a barrage ahead brought his mind back to the present situation. Artillery fire and fighter bombers were being directed on to the next line of Red Army positions discovered by air reconnaissance. The Chaffees had several miles of clear road before they reached them. The Reds had left this area devoid of heavy defensive fortifications, leaving a gap where they could conduct a counter-attack using massed armor. The allies planned to use this open ground against them, and turn the tactical possibilities on their head.

It was going to be where the tank destroyers of the 558th would be operating once they caught up with Cooper's platoon.

A mile from the Red defenses, Cooper radioed his troop. "Wideout Leader to all units, prepare to go cross country on my signal."

The terrain was ideal for an armored engagement, low rolling grassland stretching for miles in all directions. The few obstacles to unimpeded movement were the scattered creeks and eroded gullies, which provided seasonal drainage for the now subsided winter snow-melt.

"Next radio check is at sixteen hundred hours. First one to bring in the flyboys gets to shout the others a round. Good luck!"

Cooper waved his arm and the light tanks dispersed according to their assigned headings. Three-Z trundled smoothly onto the vast carpet of undulating green, and for several minutes Cooper watched the turrets of the other Chaffees as they bobbed up and down over the rolling steppe, and then disappeared in to the distance. All manned by experienced tankers, he knew that each unit would acquit themselves as well as his own.

For the next fifteen minutes Three-Z's crew went about their work in silence. Each member intently scanning their assigned direction with fingers rigid on triggers. Eyes sharpened by adrenaline, they put any weariness aside with thoughts of the next furlough.

The Chaffee slowed as it ascended a low incline, alerted eyes picking out any signs of life as they topped the rise and sighted another few square miles of unfolding greenscape, then coasted down the other side into the temporary cover between slopes.

Another slow climb, another ride downhill. And so on for half an hour.

From the commander's hatch, Cooper was also keeping a lookout on the sky. He was well aware they were in No-man's land, and their chances of being mistaken for an enemy tank by the allied air-force were increased. Coordination and communication between land and air units had improved significantly in the 3rd Army under Patton's command. All of the units in the troop were in contact with battalion HQ, who were on standby to relay any enemy contacts to the waiting air support overhead. In addition, the Chaffees could change to the designated frequency used by the fighter-bombers to either correct their targeting, or call off any misdirected fire.

The country started to turn from clean, grassy expanses to being dotted with trees and low shrubs. Another climb, more tense, watchful moments as they rolled over the top ... then the ground erupted in front of the tank – shoveling dirt and clods of earth over the hull.

"*Head for cover!*" shouted Cooper.

Greene accelerated forward into the next gully.

"Anyone see the shot?"

No reply meant no one had.

The Chaffee sped up to get off the exposed slope, and then Greene had to start a gradual swerve so they could change direction and go along the depression instead of up the next incline. Once leveled out, he got the tank up to thirty miles per hour.

Shouldn't be able to get her up to this speed down here ...

Then he noticed something about the ground they were traversing. It was hard and compacted.

He looked down and saw why ... tank tracks.

Another shell exploded not far behind them.

Greene didn't have time to call out to Cooper ... nor did he need to.

Cooper had turned around to see where the last round had come from. He could scarcely believe what he was seeing. Half a mile to their rear, the front face of a knoll was folding upwards as dozens of yards of canvas netting was being raised.

As it opened, Cooper gaped in horror, as he could see the menacing snouts of several IS2s emerging from beneath the rising camouflage.

It was an impressive piece of concealment. The netting matched the surrounding shrubbery and would have been invisible from the air.

He saw a bright flash shoot out from one of the barrels.

"Fire smoke!" he yelled, as the shell screamed past the fast-moving Chaffee.

They rounded a bend at full speed. A smattering of small-arms fire from dug-in infantry pinged off the hull.

"Stay down in this gully ..."

Whoompf!

The muffled sound of another explosion echoed inside the close confines of the turret, possibly from an AT grenade. Cooper grabbed his map and checked their position against the expected path of one of the Hellcat platoons who should be following up along behind them.

"Head south ... there's a wide channel we can take to the left coming up ahead."

The firing died down as they motored away in the direction from which they'd come.

The gully began to get shallower and a few hundred yards

ahead the trees and undergrowth started to clear on either side, making way for the open grassland beyond.

"Slow us down … I want to halt before we go out on to the steppe again so we can look around."

"We sure can't turn and fight," said Keponee. "The 75's a pop-gun against those IS2s."

Cooper swiveled his scope around, checking for any pursuers.

"Aim at their tracks if we see any more of them, at least we'd have a chance of getting away."

Greene slowed them to walking pace, and the crew scoured the slopes ahead for any signs of camouflage. The twin Cadillacs idled down to a purr, and the drop in volume seemed to coincide with lower heart rates for the crew as the adrenaline rush of the previous frantic minutes subsided.

They continued at a crawl, all eyes straining for any sign of the Soviets, then Cooper thought he heard something over the sound of the engines.

He flipped up one ear flap on his leather helmet so he could make out the sound more clearly. *There!* A deep rumbling, a throbbing that sounded like a very large … engine.

The sound grew, penetrating the air all around them … all of the crew could now hear it. Heads turned from side to side trying to locate the source of the sound … guns at the ready. Greene braked suddenly as lumbering out from the cover of trees to one side appeared the massive square turret of a metal monster.

"*KV2!*" the driver shouted.

They had nowhere to go but back.

"*Turn us around!*" Cooper yelled.

As Greene desperately reversed, the KV2 lurched into full view. A 50-ton giant, it looked like a steel blockhouse mounted on a tank chassis. Greene had no rear vision, so he backed around until he had room to execute a U-turn. Fortunately, the giant Russian tank was extremely slow at maneuvering, so he thought he could pull off the turn before they got in the Russians' sights.

The crew's heart rates went back up to emergency levels as half way through the turn, the Chaffee's weak side-armor was fully exposed to the enemy tank. One hundred yards away, the KV2 was laboriously swinging its deadly 152mm howitzer ... it was only a few degrees from pointing directly at them.

"*Move! Move! Move!*" screamed Cooper.

Greene pushed Three-Z forward just as the KV2 fired.

A massive blast of high-explosive threw up tons of dirt, smoke and flame over the little tank.

Cooper had been knocked down to the deck by the shock-wave's impact, but recovered quickly. Planting his feet wide apart so as to steady himself against the motion of the wildly lurching Chaffee, he got up and put his eye back to his scope. Behind them, he saw a trail of fuel cans, ammo boxes and spare treads that had been blown off the back of their tank.

Expecting to be accelerating away by now, Cooper could feel something was wrong.

"She's lost power ..." Greene called over his shoulder, "... can't get her past twenty ..."

Three-Z hobbled away as the huge bulk of the KV2 turned slowly on its axis toward them, its crew reloading.

The Chaffee's turret rotated around to face it. Keponee looked through his viewfinder and aimed in at the near side of the Russian tank. If he could damage one of its tracks it would immobilize them and slow them from bringing their gun to bear.

Only gonna get one shot.

He fired and watched helplessly as the smoke around the KV2 cleared.

"*Hit! They're tracked!*"

"Only slowed 'em down ..." Cooper said dismissively, as he screwed his eye up to his scope, "... they'll still be onto us in a few more seconds."

Now three hundred yards behind them, the muzzle of the

155mm howitzer inched around to line up on the limping Chaffee.

For the crew, it seemed as though there was nothing they could do. To the Chaffee's 75mm, the KV2's thick armor was impenetrable.

Keponee looked at Cooper. "Shit ..."

∞

Captain Deming checked his map. According to Wideout's last message, the Red armor would only be a mile and a half ahead. Following behind the scout tanks, the Hellcats were adhering to the new tactics and providing a block to the flank of the main thrust of the division.

While thousands of Allied troops and hundreds of T32s and T30s were slogging their way through the defenses around Krynki, four companies of the 558th along with their combat engineers, Legionnaires, and the LRDG were providing a defensive screen to their left.

The previous day, light tanks operating ahead of them had reported they'd found enemy armor, but there had been no indication of their strength. Then fifteen minutes ago, a recon flight had spotted a number of Red Army tanks moving east toward the left flank of 10th Armored Division.

Deming thought they were probably relocating for fear of being attacked by allied bombers, but as they were heading for the main body of the US division, the battalion had been called in to head them off. In addition to Deming's force, three other Hellcat companies several miles away on either side, were searching for Red Army tank columns.

This change in formation meant that Deming's tank was no longer the quarterback and now had another designation. "Running Back leader to all units, listen up ..."

He waited while the other tank destroyer commanders in his

company acknowledged, then continued, "We have confirmed enemy armor in the area, last known position five miles at our twelve o'clock, and moving on this position."

He looked at his map again.

"They should be coming at us from one of the gullies straight ahead. I want R-B One, Three and Five to flank right, Two, Four, and Six will go left. You know what to do, stay mobile, and engage the enemy on sight."

"*Shoot and scoot!*" echoed over the radio from an officer commanding one of the flanking units.

Deming scanned the surrounding terrain again, double-checking he was satisfied with his choice for his own group's position for the ambush.

"R-B Seven, Eight, and Nine are with me. Get your tanks hull-down behind the slopes around us here."

There was no need for him to give more precise orders. It was up to the commander of each Hellcat to use their own judgment, and get their own tank sighted along the enemy's expected line of approach. Deming then signaled the combat engineers and a company of Legionnaires to deploy on their flanks and cover the now stationary M18s from any enemy infantry.

The 558th had drilled for just this kind of scenario. Knowing its similarity to the type of terrain they would be fighting on, Colonel Corday's battalion had conducted exercises on the rolling plains of Poland. Fast moving groups of tank destroyers, using their mobility to out-maneuver the much slower heavy armor of the enemy. They could hit and run, using the cover between slopes to avoid the return fire. This would be how they ran the upcoming play – Deming's troop being the offensive line, and the wide receivers moving to outflank the enemy's defensive line.

Black smoke blurted out from the Hellcats' triple exhausts as the company began to deploy. The two flanking troops fanned out and soon disappeared from sight. Deming's troop assumed a hull-down profile, where they could fire upon an eight hundred-yard channel of grassland in front of them, but quickly drop back behind the cover of the sloping ground to avoid return fire.

The co-ordination between air reconnaissance and ground forces was bearing fruit. Deming received another message from HQ, the column of enemy tanks was moving directly toward them – strength estimated to be at least a brigade.

The numbers don't matter right now ... it's all about making the right plays.

As if to reinforce his point, the sound of gunfire met their ears.

"Contact!" Deming heard over the battle net, *"Two thousand yards!"*

His crew steeled for action, fears brushed aside, and every thought intent on executing their purpose – killing the enemy.

Tense seconds followed. Would the Reds keep coming on ... or would they stop to engage the attacking Hellcats?

The chatter over the radio soon told the story. The flankers on Deming's left had fired a volley at the enemy column, scoring some hits, then they'd disengaged, changing direction back toward the commander's group.

The flanking troop on the right were about to engage. They reported that the Red column was continuing along the gully.

That should bring them under our guns.

Minutes later, dull green rectangles loomed out from the long grass.

"IS2s!" Deming called over the intercom, "Fire at will!"

Geysers of earth and smoke erupted around the column's lead tanks as the four Hellcats fired as one.

Deming groaned, as through his scope he couldn't see any hits. A painstaking five seconds elapsed as they reloaded.

One more round then we'll back off.

Carrummmpff!

At less than five hundred yards, the foremost IS2's turret

exploded as a 90mm HVAP shell hit its gun mantle.

"*Hit!*" shouted Deming, "*Start rocking!*"

The Hellcat lurched backward. Russian shells screamed overhead as Deming checked that the other units in his troop had also safely backed off.

Immediately, and in unison, they rocked forward and fired another volley. Another IS2 was hit, this time by two high-velocity rounds simultaneously. Its turret blew off, spinning sideways into the grass.

The Red column faltered. Their commanders were uncertain whether to head straight at their attackers, stay in position and take careful aim ... or disperse and try to find a better position from which to return fire.

Those fatal seconds of indecision cost them more lives.

The troop of Hellcats on the right flank engaged from a low rise only two hundred yards behind the head of the column.

Another IS2 died, another two were damaged.

Turrets swiveled around in response, presenting an even better target to the guns of Deming's troop.

The carnage continued for several minutes, as the Hellcats fired relentlessly, moving in and out of cover. Some cooler-headed Russian gunners managed to score hits by taking aim and waiting for a Hellcat to come into their sights. One of Deming's squad took a hit as it rolled forward into firing position. The 122mm shell hit the front glacis plate just below the M18's turret, slicing through the light armor and hitting the ammo rack. The detonation was staggering, and exploding rounds shot out from the fireball. The crew had died instantly.

Time to bug out, thought Deming.

"*Let's move!*" he called over the battle net frequency.

"Relocate to Tango-Five ... repeat, relocate to Tango-Five!"

All armored and mounted infantry units withdrew and began moving at speed to the designated rally point five miles to the south-east.

Behind them, a dozen burning tanks sent pillars of smoke in to the clear blue sky. Only two of them were American.

That was two too many, Deming lamented, knowing the loss his crew would be feeling as they left their buddies behind.

He radioed a sitrep to headquarters and stayed on station to wait for updated orders from Corday.

The bumping ride to the rally position seemed surreal and strangely peaceful after the clamor and insanity of the firefight. No one spoke.

Deming took the time to process the experience of the battle. Had they done everything right? Did any men die because of his poor decisions?

He dismissed the questions. He knew he'd done the best he could. Then in his mind he saw the other side of the battle – the enemy's losses. He recalled each of the Red Army tanks being destroyed, and the sight of the fiery wrecks and their crews burning alive inside.

He felt nothing for them.

After all … they started it.

A few minutes later, the awaited message came through from Colonel Corday.

There was an urgency in his voice, "Captain, you've got to get your men out of there! B Company has just radioed in that they've encountered a mass of Red armor, and are executing a fighting retreat. We have not heard from any of the scout units and suspect they are no longer operational. This is looking like a major counter-attack."

Deming checked his map and could see where this was going. The Soviets were aiming at a point where the 10th Armored's flank intersected with the 26th Infantry Division to their right. He knew from the mission briefing that General Wyatt had been pushing his armor at full speed, but this had left the infantry struggling to keep up. Now the gap had widened between the two divisions.

Deming got that feeling again, the one where he and his men were about to be the rats in the maze built by the brass-hats.

A flight of allied fighter bombers roared overhead, drowning out some of Corday's words. "… going to be a hell of a fight …" is all he made out.

The Colonel didn't disappoint Deming's intuition. His voice leveled off, signifying the gravity of the situation, "Son, you've got to try to slow down any Red armor you come across … at the same time, make your way south-east to link up with 10th Armored Division. The other tank-destroyer companies will be doing likewise, so be sure to keep a watch out for them – we don't want any mistakes out there."

The sound of anti-aircraft fire thumped away in the distance as Corday finished delivering their orders, "I can't stress enough the importance of your role … the Russkies will be throwing everything they've got into this attack. If we beat them off we could open up the road to Moscow."

Deming disconnected and then passed on the briefing to his crews. Then they raced into the maze, and went looking for the cheese.

∞

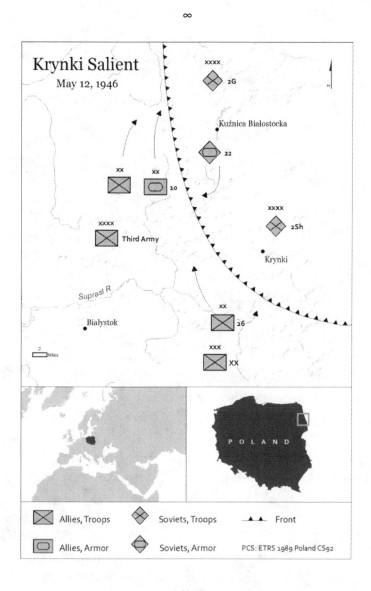

558th Tank Destroyer Battalion headquarters was in a state of controlled chaos. A constant flurry of messages was being carried back and forth between the comms section and the officers in the planning area of the ruined farm buildings.

The Battle of Krynki was in the balance. The Allied divisions comprising 3rd Army executing the encirclement of the twenty Soviet divisions of the 2nd Guards Tank Army and 2nd Shock Army, were in danger of being outflanked.

Colonel Corday, stooping over the map table, looked at his watch. They hadn't heard from their units since the morning.

"The minute any of the companies make contact, I want orders going out to the others to provide support ... and where's that air recon?"

Lieutenant Clay headed to comms to follow up.

Corday scoured the map, then grunted in frustration. The lack of updated information was going to get men killed.

He moved to the theater map on the wall, "General Wyatt has informed me that the Soviet offensive is an attempt to stop us reaching Minsk ... and to delay our drive to Moscow until winter sets in."

The group around the table watched as the Battalion Commander used a baton to draw an imaginary line heading north from the battle.

"They've concentrated more than fifty divisions across a one hundred mile front ..."

The baton waved from side to side over the map, with the key city of Minsk in the center, "... with another twenty divisions in reserve. This is good news for our campaign along the Baltic coast ..." he said, as he pointed briefly to an area around Riga in Latvia, where several Marine divisions advancing from the landings at Gdansk, had been slogging away.

"... as the Reds must have diverted some of their reserves from that region for this attack. The bad news is that those russkie divisions are now here ..." He tapped the map. "... in front of us."

He turned away from the map, and assumed the countenance of a coach getting his team ready for a really tough match.

"General Patton has called this the 'Red Brick Wall' ... but he also thinks that the thing about walls is that they're rigid, and they crumble when you make holes in them."

A stir rippled through the officers and men on hearing the 3rd Army leader's words.

"... and *we* gentlemen, along with the rest of 10th Armored Division ... will be the sledgehammer!"

A cheer went up, and the Colonel soaked up the optimism for a moment before continuing. "But for now, we'll have to hold our ground, and with the help of our air superiority, beat off this counter-attack."

Lieutenant Clay returned with an update, "Colonel, the other four companies have linked up with Alpha Company."

He stopped at the map table and indicated to an area behind a large group of red-arrow markers.

"They are engaged in a harassing action, and have also been coordinating with XIX th Tactical Air Force observers to direct fighter-bombers onto the Red armor."

"Hmmm ... sounds like the running-back is doing his job ... putting in a block ... hopefully it'll slow some of the Russkies down."

Corday looked at the map where Lieutenant Clay had just shown them where Deming was fighting. He could see that 10th Armored would only be able to continue to close off the encirclement if the infantry division covering their flank had time to move up and stop the Red armor.

It was also now clear that the main units of their battalion were cut off behind the advancing enemy.

Lieutenant Clay completed the picture he'd just put together while in the comms section. "Division has advised that the Hellcat's activities are having a double effect ... air recon reports show that the progress of the Red armored columns appears to be slowing down, probably due in part to them having to deal with the uncertainty caused by our tank destroyers in their rear."

The Operations Intelligence officer looked as though he were a cat with a mouse. "It's also having the effect of compressing these three Red columns here, here and here ... as the units at the head of those columns are unable to fan out and deploy as they were no doubt intended to do."

Corday lifted his attention from the field of operations, to a more strategic picture. "So much armor compressed in such a small area ..."

A glint in his eye showed how he relished the prospect, "I'm also going to call for air support – but from IX Air Force Bomber Command."

∞

Breathless, Cooper dropped and buried himself into the tall grass of the steppe. Keponee and Greene followed suit. The engines of the mechanized units searching for them growled and the ground shook thunderously, permeating a shudder through their bones. The knee-high grass gave them the same comfort as if it were a stone wall. It was keeping them out of sight, but that was all. The armor roaming around them would crush either as easily as if it were cardboard.

The three of them were all that remained of the Chaffee's crew of five after its encounter with the KV2. They'd spent the night hiding in a grove of trees, huddled together to keep warm under the increasing drizzle. Now they were moving south toward their own lines, through the fading green of a sea of grass turning to seed.

With the sound of engines growing louder, Cooper didn't need to signal the others to be quiet. Crouching low, his left side burned due to a chunk of shrapnel from the KV2's killer blow still stuck in his shoulder blade.

"Half-track ... *get ready!*"

The grease-gun in his right hand felt light and nimble, so he'd try to use it one-handed if they were spotted. He held up his blood-streaked left hand, signaling for the other two to hold their fire. The clanking rumble of tank treads grew deafening. Cooper threw himself lower, hugging the earth harder trying to be invisible, but coiling himself like a spring in case he had to roll out of the way.

Through the feathered veil of green, he glimpsed several of the distinctive rounded helmets of the Red Army. As he watched them bob around above the armored side of a half-track, the pounding in his heart put a painful pressure on his wounds, and he thought he might pass out.

Gotta stay on top of this ... the guys need me.

Within seconds, the rumbling passed and began to recede, followed immediately by a second vehicle, then a third. Fortunately, they were following an animal track and not spread out, line abreast. The three waited another full minute before moving off again.

"We'll head south-west. That should keep us in line with the Division's forward units."

If everything is still going to plan, he thought ... *ours sure went south after that KV2 hit us.*

Although his memory of the encounter was murky, he knew they'd only survived Three-Z's destruction because the Russian tank could only fire high-explosive shells meant for killing infantry – not other tanks.

If it'd been armor-piercing we'd all still be inside the wreck.

The pain in his shoulder was affecting his concentration; he had to strain to maintain a positive frame of mind – essential for the leader under circumstances like these.

The distance back to their own units was unknown ... maybe ten miles – maybe twenty, depending how the battle was going. With so much enemy activity it was going to be a miracle if they made it.

Better keep any doubts to myself though ... let the guys focus on keeping us alive ... I'll just do the navigating.

He looked up at the sun, their only means of finding a direction.

Gonna be dark soon ... if we find a good hole-up we'll take it.

The horizon ahead was stained by the smoke of battle. The late afternoon sun painted a gloss of gold over the dark gray of the evening, and Cooper took heart. He'd seen a hundred sunsets mark the end of the day's fighting. The night would force both sides to limit their operations to patrols and skirmishes, for fear of mistaking their own troops for the enemy.

The trio followed a heavily treed gully for a mile or so, then stopped for a rest.

"Wonder how the TDs are doing?" Greene pondered as they fell to ground beneath a big oak.

"Better than us I hope," Keponee said flatly, leaning back against the tree. "And remember they'll be getting re-supped by air."

He looked over at his wounded commander, "Coop, your arm okay?" he asked, "You want me take a look at it?"

Cooper was flat out on his back, cushioned by a carpet of sphagnum moss. All he wanted to do was fall into the painless oblivion of sleep, but he knew it was too early for that.

"Nah ... I'll just pack some of this green shit into it ... you guys keep a look out. If we don't see any Reds before it gets dark we'll stay here."

They hadn't had any time to grab a first-aid kit when the Chaffee brewed up, just guns. First rule: staying alive meant being able to fight back. Then you could worry about details like food or injuries. They couldn't do anything about either for the moment. The sooner they got back to the Division the better.

A half-hour of rest then we keep moving through the night.

As the distant drumming of artillery slowly subsided, Cooper watched with relief as the sky darkened, and the first star blinked into view. An early evening chill drifted through the air under the big tree, and he thought how much more comfortable they'd be inside the close confines of their tank.

"Damn," he complained. "Why does it feel like I just broke up with my girlfriend?"

Keponee laughed. "Hah! I'm gonna miss that little tank too."

The gunner sat up and watched Cooper wince as he stuffed moss over the wound under his shirt. He tried to distract him to help keep his mind off the pain.

"So ... your girlfriend; is she pretty?"

"Oooohhh yeah ..." Cooper said, and smiled at her memory. "Skin like a pink rose petal, hair like maple syrup ... and ..."

"Stop! Stop already ... I get the picture ... and you're making me hungry."

"Maple syrup on flapjacks ..." lamented Greene, "... maybe we could improvise – there's plenty of wheat out there on the prairie, make some flour ... smother the pancakes in oak sap ..."

"Oh shut-up man," Cooper moaned. "I thought *I* was delirious."

The thoughts of his girlfriend had helped with the pain, so he continued to revel in his memories.

"I remember the first time I took I her out," he continued. "It was the first time – you know, so I was only expecting dinner and maybe some face slapping. We went to a diner where I knew the desserts were *great*, cuz girls just *love* their dessert," he said sagely. "Anyway, like I said, not expecting anything ... but the peach cobbler must have been awesome, cuz she was all over me when I dropped her home."

"Neck injuries?"

"Man ... talk about a tongue lashing ..."

"And that's when you got your face slapped," Greene said, putting a dampener on the cozy picture.

"Hey, how else is a guy supposed to know how far to go?"

Keponee added, finishing Cooper's story. He stood up and offered his commander a hand up.

They walked carefully on in the twilight, giving their eyes time to adjust. There would be no moon, so Cooper picked out a star in the southern sky and used it as a reference.

The conversation fell to a whisper, but talking would keep them all in earshot when the darkness fully enclosed them.

"In a hushed voice, Greene asked, "So, when we get back, what are we gonna call Three-Z's replacement?"

Keponee thought for a moment, "Well, if we call her Four-Z, that ain't gonna rhyme so well as Three-Z."

Greene huffed, "And, you would also have to think of another Z – to go with the first three. I mean, Zpeed, Zwerves and Zmoke – how can we add to that?"

"We shouldn't." said Cooper seriously. "It'd be bad luck ... she's gone. We'll get a new tank with a new name. End of story."

The three continued on in silence through the gullies of the Belarussian countryside.

The gullies were the most likely place for the troops of either side to bivouac for the night. They had to stop several times to listen for sounds of movement ahead.

Through the gloom, Cooper made out signs of an encampment ahead.

He raised his hand and then pointed. *"No sound ..."*

They crept forward for a few yards, then relaxed, it was deserted. A wide area among the trees was littered with garbage and discarded equipment, abandoned in the haste of evacuating. The trio found a water drum, and filled an empty canteen. The cap leaked, but it would stay full if not turned upside-down. They rummaged through some cartons and found a packet of biscuits. Although stale, they silenced grumbling bellies, and gave the satisfaction of an unexpected find.

"Better keep moving," Cooper said as he picked up his sub-machine gun. "There's still miles to go, and we'll have a better chance of getting through the Russkie lines while its dark."

The progress in the near-total darkness was slow. For hours they followed the lines of creek beds and gullies, having to clamber up to the steppe plateau every now and then so they could get a better view of the stars and take a bearing. On one such ascent, Cooper stopped suddenly and waved the other two to get down. He thought he saw a figure in the gloom. He had to look slightly to one side of where he thought it was, so he could make out the silhouette. Then *there!*

Fifty yards away, but it was hard to gauge distance.

He hissed to the others, *"Sentry!"*

"We need to get past him, he's standing on the lip of this gully … means there's probably more of them down in the trees. We can't risk going out in the open to get around him."

Keponee moved forward and drew his knife. "He's mine."

Cooper watched the gunner crouch low and silently move off to stalk his quarry. He thought how valuable all of the additional training in recon tactics at Camp Hood had now become.

Keponee on the other hand, was thinking how all of the time spent hunting in the Canadian Rockies was now going to help him.

As the minutes passed, Cooper strained to keep his eye on the sentry. He only caught glimpses of him when he moved, and a star on the horizon would blink out before re-appearing.

C'mon Keponee …

Anxious minutes passed before a rustling heralded the gunner's return.

"He's down," Keponee said with the indifference of an assassin.

"What's there?" Cooper asked.

"Tanks. Looks like T34s."

"Those old tin cans?" Cooper whined, "They remind me a duck every time I see one … little head on a big body. They must be here in reserve – they certainly aren't their front-line armor."

He thought about just skirting around the top, but there might be more guards further ahead. Then he had another idea, "C'mon, let's go visit Ivan."

∞

Then you will know the truth, and the truth will set you free.
John 8:32

Mojave City
2266 CE

Arjon looked across from the podium to the eaves. Eya clasped her hands together in support and gave him a reassuring smile. Her husband's face appeared on the screens around the Great Hall, then he spoke, haltingly at first.

"Fellow members ... of our wonderful ... Free ... World."

His nerves calmed, bolstered by the confidence drawn from his years of courtroom oratory. Standing there, looking out into the crowded hall, and aware of the multitude that would be watching and listening, it dawned on him that they were all the same as he: like-minded and rational human beings. He wasn't about to undermine their perfect world – just try to enhance it.

"I stand before you, not as a representative of any of the Pillars of our democratic society, but as an objective outsider; an independent arbiter, so that there is no question of self-interest with respect to what I am about to disclose."

He smiled at the world, relishing this opportunity. He was delivering a message that would raise their understanding – their view of themselves, and of those who had come before them. He indicated to the huge screen behind him.

"The Four Pillars have agreed that the technology that has produced the alternative history about to be presented is as valid as any version derived and interpreted from traditional historical research ... as performed by humans."

He paused a moment to allow the audience to digest the meaning of his words, then continued. "This will be a brief excerpt from that alternative history."

Hesta's simulation, starting with General Patton's near-miss began. The summary highlighted the Cold War. The half-century of misdirected production where enough nuclear weapons were built to wipe out all life on the Earth fifty times over. The narrative told of the events that would have occurred had the Union of Nations been undermined at its founding. The communist aggression that ensued in Asia, the invasion of Tibet and the resulting genocide. The wars and military industrialization continued through to the twenty-first century, and more importantly, the simulation showed what the decades of military build-up would have cost the human race.

If those resources had been devoted to a saner purpose, the alternative humanity would have avoided the oppression of tyrannical regimes and the ongoing wars to defeat them, environmental crises, famine and other global tragedies.

For almost an hour, the world watched in stunned silence, before a collective moan signified the end of the presentation.

Arjon explained, "So you see, over two and a half centuries ago, a singular event occurred, an accident, which had it turned out differently, would have shaped our world in ways we would prefer *not* to imagine."

He glanced across to Eya, seeking confirmation that it was going well. She glowed with pride and a serene calm, which flowed between them. Drawing courage from this moment of emotional union, Arjon proceeded with his speech.

"We do *not* live in a world divided by ignorance, aggression, or any of the myriad other failings of our pre-Pillar history."

The audience before him seemed exhausted, but he managed to regain their attention, "And in one of the greatest ironies one could conceive ... we owe our perfect way of life – to the *victories* won by our ancestors ..."

Another pause, as he sensed his words may now be falling on dissenting ears. He sensed some resistance to these conclusions, but continued, "... to the foresight, resolve ... and *sacrifice*, of those who took action at a critical juncture – when the future of our world was in a perilous balance."

His closing sentence echoed out above the silent crowd, and drifted up into the vast expanse toward the Hall's smooth white ceiling. Arjon looked up, and instead of feeling enclosed inside a building, allowed his mind to roam out into the solar system. He could see humanity one day reaching to the stars, and the prosperous activity already under way on the asteroids and planets of their home system. His perspective turned back to the Earth, so small and tentative among the immensity of the universe, but also so dynamic and beautiful.

With those who had come before in mind, he called aloud, *"Thank you!"*

He bowed gracefully, then left the podium, his contribution complete.

The Orator returned to the stage.

The crowd settled, as though the Orator's established authority would help to put their minds at ease.

"The Center of Truth has verified the preceding simulation using the most advanced artificial intelligence technologies available."

That quietened any doubts within the audience.

"It follows, that the Four Pillars of our society, Sanity, Evolution, Unity ... and Truth, are in confluence with a new resolution."

A murmur ran throughout the Hall and diminished again as the Orator raised his voice.

"The Four Pillars, previously thought to encompass *all* of humanity's highest aspirations, and being the embodiment of who we are as a species, and who we wish to be ... are in need of a re-evaluation of this all-encompassing perspective."

The murmuring resumed, what did this mean? Perfect societies aren't altered with a change of direction of the wind, or the findings of a single Enlightenment.

"It is proposed that a new Pillar be founded – one which will utilize the technology demonstrated here today, to formalize a strategic direction for the Free World as we head for the stars."

"The fifth Pillar will be the Directory of Purpose. Its charter, structure and methodology will be proposed by contributions from the other Pillars, however, as determined by the purest form of democracy, its final form will be approved by citizen referendum."

A spontaneous cheer erupted. The good sense of the proposal was instantly recognized. A Pillar to guide humanity, working with the assistance of the other Pillars, it seemed so simple – why hadn't it happened before now?

"In addition, and in honor and recognition of those recently confirmed to be instrumental in the founding of our Free World, there will be a new flag for the Union of Nations – also to be chosen by referendum."

On the screens, several images appeared. At their center, most conspicuous and seemingly the most likely to be selected, was an ensign comprised of a navy-blue background, with a circle of silver stars. Each star represented one of the pillars, with the fifth star also being cognizant of the five-star General featured so prominently in the latest Enlightenment.

∞

Krynki Salient,
May 13th, 1946
0330 HRS

"What the hell are all these pedals for?" Greene whispered in the dim glow of the T34's battery lighting.

Cooper leant through and pointed to each one "Fuel injection, clutch, brake ..."

"Ok I got it ... what about that one?"

"*Don't touch that!*" Cooper seethed, "It's the Desantov – it sets off a device that disables the tank."

"You're kidding me? This bucket of bolts has a self-destruct button?"

Keponee was inspecting the gun aiming mechanism. He asked Cooper, "Hey, how come you know so much about this tank?"

"I was at Aberdeen Proving Grounds in '42 when we tested an earlier model, and that one was even more cramped that this."

The gunner was peering around the interior of the turret, counting the 75mm ammunition, "Hey, I only see nine rounds – where's the rest?"

"You're standing on it," Cooper replied as he looked through the commander's periscope. Totally dark as expected – it was still hours till dawn. They'd chosen a T34 on the southern outskirts of the tank park with no significant obstacles preventing them getting a clean exit up on to the steppe.

They turned off the interior lights so no light would show when they opened the hatches.

"Don't turn on the headlights unless we absolutely have to – we don't want to give them a target to shoot at."

Greene nodded, and silently opened the driver's hatch. Popping his head out, it was completely dark under the camouflage netting draped between the trees. He knew that unseen sentries were all around, they'd bypassed several while creeping through the tank park.

After waiting a few minutes for his eyesight to adjust, he could make out the barely discernible lightness of the sky above the horizon to the east. Then he made out the lighter shade of the trail leading out of the trees, and up to the flat grassland above.

He gave a thumbs-up to signal his readiness, then when there was no response, he realized no one could see his gesture.

"*Ready,*" he whispered.

A slap on his shoulder gave him the go-ahead.

The tank's engine roared to life, and Greene pushed hard on the control levers. The tank lurched forward, chased by the sound of shouts of alarm from the guards.

At first, the startled soldiers weren't sure who was responsible for the T34's sudden departure, so no shots were fired. An officer roused from his tent immediately thought it was a desertion, and so began giving orders for a pursuit.

Cooper flipped open his hatch to get a better look, but found it opened forwards, and blocked any view in that direction.

Shit, how the hell do the goddammed Reds see where the hell they're going?

He leaned out sideways, then without helmet intercom, had to yell down to Greene to be heard over the din of the engine, "Straight ahead for a hundred yards, if the gully branches off, follow it to the right!"

"Kep, swing the turret forty-five degrees so I can see where we're going!"

As Greene pushed them up to twenty miles per hour, the duck head turret swiveled around. Cooper could now make out the ground further ahead. He saw the lighter-colored patches of grassland, leading up to a black expanse.

"Greene!" he shouted urgently. "Gully! Turn! NOW!"

The driver pulled with all his might on the sluggish levers and the chassis moaned from the effort. The T34 slowed and turned in time, causing a small landslide to release from the top lip of the gully.

Hundreds of yards behind them, two tanks lumbered off in the vain hope of catching them, or even sighting them in the darkness.

Cooper wasn't worried about any pursuit from behind. What

worried him more was what lay ahead. They had to find the main road back toward Krynki, or risk running into trenches filled with Russian infantry, minefields, anti-tank guns ... he had to stop himself thinking about the possibilities and to focus on keeping them on course. For the first time in an hour, he felt the pain in his shoulder flaring up, aggravated by the vibration through the rumbling tank.

At least it'll help me stay awake.

Half an hour later, the lightening sky was making it harder to pick out the star they'd been following.

Greene suddenly accelerated, snapping the others out of their dull half-sleep.

"Man up!" he shouted.

A whooshing sound surrounded the tank, followed by a hollow repetitive snapping.

"What is that?" Cooper called to his driver.

"A tent!" answered Greene, "Here's another one!"

This time the whoosh – slap, was accompanied by a gentle bumping. Bodies, asleep – never to awaken.

They motored on through the infantry camp, not hearing the commotion they left behind.

Minutes later, the first bluish glow of dawn seeped up from the eastern horizon.

Good, direction confirmed.

"Stay sharp! The Reds'll be getting their breakfast soon," said Cooper.

A flat land sprinkled with shrubs and a few trees spread out for miles on either side. Straight ahead, he could make out something else, something not at place with the natural contours of the land. Enemy lines.

Cooper instinctively reached for his field glasses which usually hung around his neck, but they weren't there. As his good hand groped at his chest for a second, he sighed with the realization that they'd been lost along with the Chaffee.

What he wouldn't have given to be able to stop and zoom in on the obviously heavily defended plain ahead of them.

"Close hatches."

He dropped down and closed his own hatch. The scene through the periscope gave him the feeling of being in a fish tank. The world outside was slightly out of focus, and being surrounded by so many enemy they might as well have been in a fragile box made of glass.

As they got closer, Cooper got Greene to slow down so they would attract less attention. Through the scope, he could make out a criss-crossing network of earthworks – trenches fronted by barbed-wire, and then a concrete bunker another hundred yards away. Nearby, a group of soldiers stood up out of their weapon pit and began waving.

"Just keep rolling through ... remember there's a red star on the turret."

Keponee, his face pushed up against the gunsight, grinned at the reception they were getting, "Huh, this piece of crap must be reminding them of Stalingrad ..."

Cooper swung his scope to the forward view. His pulse quickened as he saw an officer step out on to the dirt road and raise his arm.

"Greene ..."

"I see him."

"Ok ... let's start slowing down as though we're about to stop ..."

"Ya sure? What'll that look like when we go right through him?"

Cooper pictured the scene in his mind: a tank slows down then suddenly speeds up to go through an officer hailing it to stop. He could see Greene's point.

"You're right, better if it looks as though we just don't see him ... maintain this speed. *Everyone ready – pick your targets!*"

The latter command had just been a reflex ... one for a full crew of five including a bow gunner. Then he remembered there were only three of them.

He searched the approaching defenses through his scope, "Kep! 57mm AT dug in at ten o'clock! Take him out first, then choose your own targets."

The overweight duck sailed past more waving troops. The officer, an NKVD political commissar intending to check why a valuable T34 belonging to the victorious 2nd Guards Tank Army, appeared to be heading straight toward the American lines on a suicide mission.

He started waving frantically. When he realized that the tank wasn't slowing for him, he pulled out his pistol and started firing into the air.

"Buckle up boys!" Cooper shouted.

The officer lowered his hand-gun, dumbfounded, and feeling embarrassed in front of the surrounding troops at the lack of a response.

Thirty tons of unstoppable ironclad bore down on him as though he didn't exist.

At the last second, he jumped out of the way to avoid being crushed. The soldiers nearby broke out laughing, but quickly stopped when the despised and feared NKDV man raised his gun again.

Cooper swung his scope around. "They must have bought it, there's no ..." and then cut himself off as he saw something in the distance.

It couldn't be ...

Several dark green shapes were lumbering down the same track they'd been following.

How the heck did they follow us?

Then he increased focus and noticed they weren't T34s. *Look like early ISs, either a bad coincidence, or someone who spotted us radioed ahead and let them know where we were headed. No matter ...*

"Greene, step on it! Those Ivans want their tank back!"

Looking forward again, he could see the thin brown strip of dirt road meandering through some denser underbrush a mile or so ahead. It wouldn't conceal them completely but they would be a more difficult target.

"Be sure to stay on the road, there's more cover up ahead."

Still no one firing at them. Cooper scanned the middle distance. Through the viewport's glass, the glare of the early morning sun illuminated a layer of fog lying low to the ground in a depression. On either side of the road, the trenches and wire had given way to open ground, sure to be strewn with mines.

He was thinking furiously, about the next few hundred critical yards. Should they get off the road? Would it be mined out here beyond the trench lines?

But something else was nagging at him.

Greene had to slow the T34 right down as they rumbled through the patch of fog, to ensure they didn't stray off into the minefield. The crew knew that the tanks behind them would be catching up.

As Cooper anxiously waited for the sound of an incoming shell, he scoured the brush-covered terrain now only hundreds of yards up the road. If the Reds had been preparing to counter-attack through here, then the road would have been cleared of mines. They had to risk it.

The fog was clearing as the road started rising up the gentle slope out of the depression. Cooper turned the scope back to the rear. The group of Russian tanks was now amongst the trench lines, and well within range, but they were slowing down. *I've got a bad feeling about this ....*

He could see the lead IS, come to a halt. *Taking aim.*

The ugly black snout of its gun was pointing directly at them.

But they didn't fire. Cooper's sense of foreboding only increased. *Why haven't they fired? I guess they're still not sure about us.*

He called back over his shoulder, "See anything?"

"Like what?" answered Greene in frustration, "A farewell party?"

A massive thump rocked the T34. It swerved off the road out of control. Greene braked to avoid running into any mines.

"*What was that?*" Cooper asked as he swiveled around, desperately searching all around.

"Track's hit!" Greene called out, "I can't steer ..."

The driver tried to get the tank moving again, but stopped when he saw the broken track peeling off the drive sprocket and out onto the ground in front of him.

Another round thudded into the soft dirt only feet away.

"That was a six-pounder ... they're our guys!" yelled Keponee.

Cooper's mind reeled. He had to be able to think clearly, but the impact and swerve off-road had thrown him against the turret lining. The jagged piece of shrapnel in his shoulder jabbed him as though it were a serrated knife and he almost passed out from the agony.

Through clenched teeth he asked, "Anyone see any white cloth?"

They could try and make it to the allied lines to surrender, but unless they showed intent, the chances were they would just get machine-gunned.

Precious seconds passed as they frantically rummaged through lockers and under stools. Nothing.

Cooper sat back against the turret in an attempt to recover his strength. A few seconds later he had another idea, but it was one that might be riskier than just baling out, "Kep, rotate the turret, target the nearest IS."

Keponee gave him an incredulous look. Any second they could get lit up like a firework by their own army, and the commander wanted to pick a fight with the Reds.

Seeing the fresh blood streaking down Coopers arm, he wasn't going to argue, so he complied.

"... and load HE," Cooper added, "I want to make a lot of

noise."

The 75mm gun started slowly turning toward the group of halted tanks. After it had almost completed its turn, sparks crackled and burst out of a control box next to the gunner. The turret stopped dead, the gun pointing only a few degrees short of its intended angle.

"Shit!" Cooper spat, "Goddammed useless Slav engineering!"

He winced in pain from the effort of getting angry, "… and it hasn't even been raining!"

The atmosphere inside the T34 was electric from the extreme tension and irony of their situation.

Keponee urgently looked through the sight to see how close the gun had lined up to their target, "It's no good, we're gonna miss it by yards."

Cooper screamed, "I don't care if we *hit* anything … I just want a damned explosion!"

The gun fired. The shot skewed off to one side – a complete miss, but the explosion among the trenches would have been clearly visible.

"There! *Satisfied*?"

Cooper ignored him, and Keponee began to reload. The commander was waiting for a reaction – from either side. He struggled to his feet and looked through the scope. An hour seemed to pass, but it was only moments later that he got the answer he was looking for. He saw a puff of smoke from one of the ISs, and braced himself as the round slammed into the back of the engine.

Within seconds, flames began to reach through into the crew compartment. Cooper hoped like hell that the allies had seen everything, and had decided they were not the enemy.

"*Out! Out! Out!*" he shouted.

Hatches flew open and the three tumbled out. They sprinted back on to the road and started zig-zagging. Spurts of dust sprang up around them to the *zip! zip! zip!* of bullet impacts. The

Russian tanks were now machine-gunning, but accuracy was impossible from such a long range.

Cooper held his damaged left arm tight against his chest to limit its movement. He couldn't keep up with the other two, but urged them on when they turned around to check on him.

The sound of artillery shells screaming overhead signaled the US Army's response, the start of another day's firefight.

Keponee looked behind and saw the shells landing in front of the trench lines. He slowed and waited for the struggling Cooper to catch up, then slung an arm around his waist to help him along.

Every dirty brown yard was another gasping second of cheating death.

Then the machine-gunning stopped as the Russian tanks started backing out of range of the artillery.

Minutes later the three slowed to a jog as they entered the protection of sparsely treed undergrowth.

A shout hailed them, "Hands up! *Rooch! Vearkh!*"

It was a GI, calling out in bad Russian – the survivors of Three-Z's crew had made it back.

∞

Rather than it should have failed, I would have seen half the earth desolated. Were there but an Adam and an Eve left in every country, and left free, it would be better than as it now is.
Thomas Jefferson

General George S. Patton sighed.

As he looked out over the smoke-clouded plain, it was a sigh of frustration rather than regret. In previous wars he'd led men into battle as a fighting man ... these days he had to lead by inspiration more than through action.

He detected no scent from the smoke and dust, which were

no doubt laden with the smell of grass-fires, burning oil and death. Over the years his senses had dulled to the acridity of the battlefield, so it was just like breathing normal air.

Lowering his field glasses from the horizon, a gust of cold swept over him. He felt gratified, rather than uneasiness, as he recognized a familiar presence.

Although Napoleon had reached Moscow in 1812, it had been a hollow victory. After continually retreating as they were fearful of a full engagement, the Russians had preferred to burn their own capital rather than allow it to be of use to the enemy.

We won't be letting them do that to us ...

He heard the faintest whispering in his ear: *glory denied by an enemy's cowardice is still a victory for honor!*

A movement from behind stirred him back to the present.

"General?"

It was Colonel Corday. "We received a report from our units operating in the enemy's rear. The operation appears to have met its objectives ... the Red Army advance is slowing."

"Excellent Colonel," the General said, turning from the battlefield, "Their efforts will have been of great strategic value." He summarized the campaign's progress, "The advancing enemy armor had been attempting to relieve the numerous Red Army divisions of the two Tank Armies being encircled by 3rd Army around Bialystok and Krynki. In all, more than forty Soviet divisions are either trapped within the salient, or confined to a fifty-mile front behind and either side of them."

It had been a huge gamble by the Red Army, similar to the one attempted by the Nazis in the Ardennes at the end of 1944. In this case, the Soviets had been pushed back from Germany, through Poland, and were now facing defeat on the border of their homeland. Stalin had ordered an all-out offensive to prevent Minsk from being taken.

The Stavka high command knew that the territory around Bialystok was the key. Defeat the Allies there, and they could retake Poland, swing west and threaten the landings on the Baltic coast.

"The efforts of your battalion, and others across the front, have, by slowing down their counter-attacks, helped to contain the enemy in the pocket, and also behind and either side of it," Patton explained.

"I appreciate the valor and sacrifice of your men. Their efforts will have a far more significant impact than the direct influence of their actions."

"Thank you sir, their losses have been heavy. Can we now send the order for the remaining units to withdraw?"

Patton sighed ... this time it was out of resignation.

"Not yet. They need to maintain their pressure a while longer."

He lifted his gaze to the heavens. "Our deliverance will soon be forthcoming."

∞

Captain Deming's Hellcat looked as though it would have to be scrapped rather than repaired.

Blackened and scarred from days spent out among the fires covering the burning steppe, high-explosive near-misses, and scores of hits from small arms fire, the M18 limped along at well below its top speed.

Just keep us moving away and out of here girl ... it won't be much longer.

He glanced at his map, his eyes straining to focus due to his recurring concussion. *We should be on the edge of the grid reference ... another half-mile should do it.*

He looked up and his gaze cleared. The sky was a brilliant azure, so clear that Deming thought he could see all the way up to the edge of space. All the way up to the realm of angels.

It was a beautiful vision, one so far removed from the

hellscape around him he almost lost touch with his reality. The reality in which he'd lost a lot of his men. If there were any other survivors, they were scattered and miles away, out of radio contact, and making their own way back.

As he watched the sky, something moved into its unreachable tranquility, and slapped him in the face.

A tiny, distant speck; a momentary glint. He squinted against the glare, and his pulse quickened.

The bright metallic pinpoint grew as the seconds passed, leaving a long contrail. It was as though the time remaining before the end of the world was being measured by a single silver line.

Deming was mesmerized, watching the line continue to stretch. He exhaled, realizing he'd been holding his breath. His heart started hammering against his chest – more silver contrails appeared – then a hundred.

"Get us out of here!"

The sky was filling with countless high-altitude bombers.

He called down to the crew inside the tank, *"Give it everything she's got! Bombers! They're ours – and there's a lot of 'em!"*

The Hellcat's engine screamed in anguish as dirty black smoke belched from the exhausts.

Deming looked up with his glasses again. The sky beneath the planes was darkening, so much that Deming wiped his grease-slicked brow thinking that it was caused by the grimy residue seeping into his vision. He was wrong.

It was the most dreadful sight he'd seen in all his life.

A black rain.

Locust swarms of steel-jacketed death growing blacker … and closer.

Bombs away.

Deming could only look up in despair. The clouds appeared to be falling straight toward them. The black clouds across the sky then formed into dark-gray sheets as they got closer to the earth, the bombs blurring as their velocity increased.

Then the first deep grumble of impacts reached his ears. He hadn't heard any whistling through the air – the first hits must have been a couple of miles off.

Maybe I can only see the leading wing ... there could be bombs dropping everywhere for miles back there ...

Three miles behind them, mayhem was erupting. The 22nd and 156th Guards Tank Armies, which had been halted in their advance while attempting to relieve the Red Army divisions being encircled around Krynki, were being wrecked.

Forty divisions – fifteen hundred tanks, thousands of guns and artillery, and hundreds of thousands of men ... either dug in or on the move – it wasn't going to make a difference.

Three thousand allied aircraft delivered the largest volume of high-explosives into one area in a single day that the world had ever seen.

Deming and his crew could hear – and feel, the continuous quaking thunder as they moved slowly away from the kill zone. Several times in the following hour, they had to release purple smoke grenades to identify themselves to low-flying fighter bombers.

The rocket-firing Thunderbolts, Mitchell bombers and numerous other types of ground-attack aircraft, had to carefully time their sorties between the waves of heavy bombers far above.

It was a day of unprecedented destruction. If it was Judgment Day, then the sentence was death.

By nightfall, it was though an atomic bomb had been dropped, and the Battle of Krynki was effectively over.

∞

New York Times
September 24th, 1946

"SOVIETS PUSH ALLIES BACK!"

"The Red Army has staged a determined counter-offensive in the Caucasus. It is estimated that they have committed up to thirty recently formed divisions in an effort to protect their major oilfields. The commander of the Allied armies facing them, General Hurley, has described the situation as "in the balance."

"The Reds are fighting desperately to defend Stalin's home country of Georgia. Their new divisions appear to have been drawn from Kazakhstan and other regions of Russia farther east. Although we have lost some previously hard-fought ground, we will be falling back to prepared defensive lines and with strong air and naval support expect to hold Rostov and the Crimea."

∞

Washington Post
November 2nd, 1946

"ALLIES BOGGED DOWN!"

"The advance on Moscow has slowed due to the increasing bad weather, turning the unsealed roads to rivers of mud. The autumn rainy season, or "Rasputitsa" (roadless season), has meant that supplying the forward armies has increasingly been conducted by rail and air.

On the other side of the front line, mass desertions of Soviet troops have been reported following a rain of a different kind. Millions of leaflets have rained down on the demoralized Soviet armies, compelling them to join the Russian Liberation Army, led by General Andrey Vlasov. It is expected General Vlasov's army, currently fighting in the vicinity of Tula, south of the capital, will have the honor of being first to enter the city when

Moscow falls."

∞

Mojave City
2266 CE

Thiessen met Arjon and Eya as they left the wing of the stage in the Great Hall.

"We should be thanking *you* Arjon," he said, "It is a measure of our society that an individual can spark a change that begins something bigger than all of us."

"It has been an honor … one I can't yet put into context. I feel that much more will arise from this."

"Of course, and so much more to arise from our new Pillar – Purpose."

After their drinks were refreshed, Arjon gave Eya a knowing look. He felt as though their relationship was symbolic of everything that had occurred. From their union, life continued. New life, the generations to follow, would then acknowledge them and what they'd accomplished, just as society was now acknowledging its beginnings.

He thought for a moment, and then asked Thiessen, "What if it was all the other way around?"

"How do you mean?" Thiessen responded.

"Our existence seems to be spent looking at the universe in a negative light, with nature as a form of chaos, and our knowledge and wisdom as peace and order – holding it at bay."

"I see. You are wondering how the human condition would be affected if the converse were true?"

"Yes, if our universe was, and always will be, a peaceful and safe environment. Would we have evolved differently? Would humans be a negative and chaotic element, destroying the universal harmony simply by existing within it?"

"Hmmm ... we humans as the serpents in the garden? I cannot answer sufficiently – I expect it may be the case. Life itself appears to be a platform for some greater purpose. Being human, living and then dying, may simply be a step in some timeless process. Perhaps one day we will be able to construct a simulation of such immense power that we could speculate on this, and derive some higher meaning."

"Well ... I hope one day to be witness to such an Enlightenment."

∞

December 9th, 1946
North of Tula, Russia

Large flakes of snow splashed against the windscreen of a staff car. The driver pulled over, got out and poured gasoline over the ice-locked wiper blades to free them. A continuous flow of trucks carrying troops rumbled past heading north.

In the back of the car, General Vlasov looked up from his notes. On the other side of the road, a column of Red Army prisoners stretched for a mile out of the whitening gloom. A low thumping of artillery fire, muffled by the conditions, rose above the idling engine. It was hard to tell from how far away, but he knew the front line was only a few miles ahead.

The prisoners moving away from the front were unconcerned by the barrage, or the hundreds of troop transports rumbling past them on the frozen road. Their war was over. Downcast and hollow eyed, they filed past, not seeing the architect of their predicament.

The car started again and Vlasov returned to his notebook and maps. His RLA was now over two hundred thousand strong, bolstered by continual recruiting from the hordes of prisoners such as those across the road. They had taken the strategic town of Tula the previous week, after a month-long battle.

Moscow lay less than fifty miles ahead. The thought of the capital being only an hour's drive away sent a warm thrill through his heart. Taking the city would be more than just the end of the war … it would spell the end of the Bolsheviks and decades of brutal oppression.

Away to his left, the dark line of the Tula-Moscow rail link followed the road. Black sleepers and steel contrasted starkly with the surrounding white-scape. It would soon be in service again, bringing armor and supplies to his army.

He looked across at the prisoners again. They were from the 144th Rifle Division of the 1st Shock Army. One of the armies that had defended Moscow from the Nazis. Their commander, Field Marshal Georgy Zhukov had also been in command of the capital's defense five years earlier. The irony of the situation struck Vlasov. The re-activation of the 1st Shock Army was no doubt a last-ditch measure taken by Stalin in the hope it would counter the Red Army's flagging morale. That he had also reinstated Zhukov as commander of Moscow's defense, further reinforced that logic, as the dictator had banished him to obscurity in Odessa due to him being too strong a political rival.

Vlasov pictured the opposing commander. A highly decorated soldier and Hero of the Soviet Union. *And how would you see me? As a soldier doing his duty? Or a traitor leading a band of criminals? No matter, the next few weeks will decide how history sees us both.*

A movement out the car window caught his eye. A wounded prisoner fell out of the column and collapsed. No one tried to stop and help him – they knew he was too weak to go on and would soon freeze to death. And so the relentless march into captivity continued.

The general wished he could stop and offer some assistance, not just to the fallen soldier, but to all of them. Some words that would give them hope, and revive their spirits.

Soon enough brothers, you will hear the truth about the evil you have been fighting for.

Their plight may be a difficult one, but he thought how different it would be if the tables were turned. If it were he and his men who were the prisoners, they wouldn't be marching to freedom, but to slave labor or execution.

Half an hour later Vlasov reached the HQ of the RLA's 2nd Division. The sounds of battle increased, and the low thump of artillery had become a rolling thunder. A meeting with the divisional staff wasn't due to begin for another hour, so Vlasov waved the driver on to tour the front lines. A short drive along a snow-covered track found them at a regimental command post. A surprised colonel greeted Vlasov, and took him to a vantage point where he could view the current battle's progress.

From a low hilltop, the officers watched the progress of an RLA attack on Red Army positions that had begun early that morning. Through his field glasses and the falling snow, Vlasov saw several dark shapes lumbering toward the enemy trenches: Sherman tanks. Each was leading a column of infantry through breaches in the barbed wire.

As they passed through the wire, the infantry with fixed bayonets, fanned out and swarmed into the Red Army trenches.

The division commander had advised Vlasov that they were facing the 18th Guards Rifle Division. These were not the half-hearted defenders who were readily surrendering – these were the die-hard communists who were fighting to the death.

On the plain below, one of the RLA soldiers, Corporal Sergei Gromynki, leapt into the bottom of an enemy trench and looked up. Further along he saw several Red Army soldiers raising their weapons at him. As he lifted his Garand M1 to fire, the staccato sound of an automatic rifle firing over his head nearly deafened him. The BAR gunner from his own unit standing above him scored some hits, but the enemy still fired back. As Corporal Gromynki fired his own weapon, he heard the sound of bullets cutting through the air around him, and also thumping into the BAR gunner.

A dead weight fell on top of Gromynki and threw him off his aim. He missed his target, a big Soviet NCO with a sub-machine gun twenty yards away. A grenade exploded behind the NCO, and he turned to see that all of his comrades were dead. Screaming with rage, he charged at the RLA soldier.

Gromynki desperately tried to free himself from under the dead BAR gunner so he could bring his gun to bear. The rushing NCO fired off his last few rounds and bullets sprayed around the RLA corporal and into the body lying on top of him. With a surge Gromynki shrugged the weight off his back and brought the rifle up to his shoulder. He got off two rounds into the charging torso, but the big man didn't break stride and kept coming. Then Gromynki heard the "*clang*" of his magazine ejecting. Out of ammo.

As the NCO closed the last few yards and leapt through the air, Gromynki lifted his rifle and jammed the stock into the ground below his shoulder. The Red Army soldier couldn't change direction in mid-air and landed on the point of Gromynki's bayonet. Ribs splintered, and a loud groan sounded as the blade pierced the NCO's chest and split his heart in two.

Corporal Gromynki got up and looked at the carnage around him. A pause for a second to acknowledge his dead comrade, then he picked up his rifle and started toward the next enemy trench.

Watching from up on the hill, Vlasov had seen this kind of scene play out many times before. The thick snow prevented him from seeing much detail, but he knew that his men were killing and dying in desperate close-pitched combat.

He sighed, and his head dropped, looking at the ground. Perhaps being on Russian soil so close to Moscow and seeing this slaughter – with the end so near, was taking its toll.

The bright white snow beneath his feet was covering the earth of his homeland, but out on the battlefield he knew, it was stained bright red with the blood of his men.

∞

Moscow
January 13th, 1947

"Do svidanya!"

Glasses clinked, and as the vodka warmed his throat, Valentin Rhuzkoi remembered the cold of a thousand winter days kept at bay by such a toast. Outside, an afternoon snow-storm was brewing, and snow was already piling up against the wooden window sill.

"Thank goodness we are not still out there."

The same thought occurred to his drinking partner, "You got that right." said Blackett, thinking of the recent months battling across barren and frozen wastes. "We were cutting it pretty fine at the end there."

The last weeks of 1946 had seen some of the bitterest fighting of the war. The retreating Red Army had defended to the last around their capital, and the Allied supply lines had been stretched to their limit. But air power had been the decisive factor, the advantage that had allowed the forces of the free world to succeed where previous armies had failed. It was not just the Allied air-force's overwhelming destructive power that reigned from above, but also its capacity to airlift the constant flow of supplies needed at the front.

"*Da*, close … very close my friend."

"I'd never been so glad to be freezing my butt off in an M40 command car, as long as it kept those goddammed muddy roads frozen over."

Rhuzkoi waved at the barman to have another round sent over. "Perhaps if it had not been their own countrymen at the gates of the city, the Bolsheviks would have fought to the last man."

Blackett nodded, gravely aware that the onset of the Russian winter had been the deadline for success. If the momentum had been stalled, and the war dragged on into another year, the risk of the Red Army building up reserves to launch counter-offensives would have greatly increased. Under the leadership of Patton and other like-minded generals, the attacking had never stopped. The first to reach Moscow, General Vlasov's RLA forces had paused long enough to allow the Red Army to vacate the city, saving it from destruction. That the capital had been spared was due as much to the will of the Muscovites, whose rioting and calls for Vlasov had "encouraged" Stalin to leave. The dictator's whereabouts were still unknown.

The OSS Colonel watched the passers-by out in the worsening snow-storm.

If only you knew. As far as you and rest of the world knew, the Bolsheviks had started the war.

He toasted. "To General Patton!"

"*Za zdorovya*! To old Blood and Guts!"

"… and to his fifth star!" added the Colonel and they finished downing their glasses. "So, what now?"

"For me? I have been offered a post in the temporary government."

"Under Vlasov?"

"It is only until the formation of the new democratic republic is completed. We will have a new constitution ... to be based on General Vlasov's Prague Manifesto."

Blackett raised his glass in recognition, having heard of the document which outlined the reforms that would end Bolshevism in Russia.

Rhuzkoi tipped glasses, and explained, "*Da,* my friend, your people know of the evils of collectivism, and of the millions who starved under the oppressive state that implemented it."

Blackett just nodded, he could tell Valentin needed to get something off his chest.

"A move to popular government, and the return of the farms and trades to the people," he said angrily.

As tears welled up, the thought of years of purges, forced labor, and the use of terror by the government to control its people, brought a wave of anguish to the farmer's son from the Ukraine. He took a swig of vodka to calm himself.

"*Boze moi* ... to read such a list of reforms ... it makes very clear what kind of state existed for these remedies to be necessary."

Another round of drinks arrived as the weather worsened, and the snow blew in flurries past the window.

The Russian brightened as he thought beyond the next few months, and continued, "After my work is done here I shall return home to the Ukraine, perhaps restore my family's farm. We shall see. I am very tired."

Blackett eyed his friend closely, the lines on his face had creased noticeably in recent months. The war, and the weather had taken its toll.

"Colonel," Valentin said thoughtfully, "I have had much time to think over the past days, after the outcome became inevitable ... but, why were your countrymen so willing to fight for our cause?"

Where is this going? thought Blackett.

"The Allied countries were weary of fighting after the hellish years of war against the Nazis. The same for Russia ... the same problems afflicted both sides ... low morale, dwindling popular support to maintain armies of any size ... and yet your Allies managed to produce as numerous a force as that which you had before VE Day?"

Blackett turned his glass around in his fingers thoughtfully. After a minute, he decided he could trust his friend with what he knew.

"Valentin, as you know there was a lot of *convincing* required ... a lot of, shall we say *guiding* the opinion of those in power."

"As did we my friend – as you know, there was the letter that General Vlasov provided to you."

"Ah yes ... the letter. We referred to it as 'The Order' when we passed it on."

"So, it seems we each only know part of the story ..."

"Okay, you spill yours and I'll spill mine."

"Please ... you first, I insist."

Blackett looked around to check that no one was within earshot, "There were several significant incidents in the months leading up to the war."

He leveled a stony look at the Russian, and Rhuzkoi understood he would never be able to repeat what he was about to hear.

"The V2 rocket plans stolen by the Soviets at the end of the war with the Nazis, and more importantly, the plot surrounding the Manhattan Project; they were engineered, the situations manipulated, so they would sway public opinion."

Rhuzkoi sighed, "Of course ... no wonder. Ha! Nothing would have been more frightening than Stalin getting the Bomb!"

Blackett added quietly, "When I say *engineered,* in the case of the plot to steal the plans for the A-Bomb, that was also partly due to Patton's influence. Once Congress and the Administration were convinced of the threat posed by the Reds, certain ongoing investigations were conducted with more enthusiasm."

Another round was delivered.

"So, you mentioned the letter?" Blackett asked leadingly.

"*Da*, you should know how it came to be ..."

"I agree ... in fact I've been tasked to find out more about it ... it's very convenient we're both sitting here having this drink."

"Tasked? By who?"

"Major, you know the OSS is in the business of knowing everything it can ... but in this case, we need to be absolutely sure of the letter's validity ... for General Patton's sake."

"I see, you need to be sure it is genuine, in case questions are asked by your government."

"Yes, we just need a more detailed explanation of how the Order eventuated. You see, General Patton is an officer of the highest honor – and I'm sure you understand we need to maintain that honor with respect to all of our past dealings."

"Yes Colonel, I understand. I also believe General Vlasov would appreciate your concerns, and would approve if I explained."

It was though both men had suddenly sobered up, and the air of camaraderie between them was now one of pure business.

"I assure you the document is genuine. We obtained the letter, this Order, a written directive from Marshal Timoshenko himself, to the Commander of the 2nd Ukrainian Front, General Ivan Fedyuninsky."

Rhuzkoi's chest lifted with pride as he continued, "That directive was in response to information that we *engineered* to fall on to Timoshenko's desk."

"We?"

"Yes Colonel, the RLA has had many friends in all sectors of Russian society. Remember, they helped your OSS with General Vlasov's escape from captivity by the Soviets when he was being brought to Moscow in 1945."

Blackett was concerned. If there had been any impropriety with the Order's creation, there could be serious ramifications later.

Vlasov read his expression and continued. "You may describe our activities as espionage, but since we are Russian citizens, we see it as internal politics."

"Politics?"

"Yes. We gave information to the NKVD. Accurate and truthful information, that your Allied armies would attack the Soviet Union in Czechoslovakia – Prague to be precise."

Blackett was dumbfounded. "You *told* them ...?"

"*Da* ..." added Rhuzkoi with infuriating indifference, "We intercepted a drop used by British couriers passing information to the Kremlin. It was considered to be a most reliable source. We replaced the contents of the drop point with our own communique. It detailed the forthcoming attack plans ... *your* attack plans, which were given credence by the 3rd Army maneuvers on the Austrian border."

Blackett took a big swig from his vodka while the Major let him digest what he'd just disclosed. It was plausible. Stalin had been paranoid about the Western allies. He'd resisted the formation of the United Nations, believing it to be a vehicle for undermining communism, and his hold on power. The negotiations at the Yalta and Potsdam conferences during the war against the Nazis had been exercises in working out who would control the post-war states. Those determinations had been implemented by the actual occupation of territories, with the bulk of Eastern Europe going to the Soviets. Stalin had deceived the other leaders by promising to hold democratic elections in return for outcomes favorable to his country, and he knew the Allies were resentful.

Once covertly receiving the plans of the Allied attack, Stalin would no doubt have leapt to the idea that they could actually go through with it. It would make perfect sense for the Allies to start another war – after all, they had the Bomb.

Minutes passed while Rhuzkoi let Blackett process what he'd just heard. Feeding the Russians information on the Allied offensive may have helped conceal the preparations by the RLA before they moved on Linz or Jihlava. The Red Army would have been focused on 3rd Army, and not been monitoring the mountains of Soviet-occupied Austria. The Colonel looked up as another question sprang to mind, "Can I ask you how you came to possess a copy of the response? The directive from Timoshenko to Fedyuninsky?"

"That, Colonel, is a story for another day ... suffice it to say that Bolshevism has many opponents in all levels of the military. It was a relatively simple matter for us to obtain such a copy of the internal order and then deliver it you."

Blackett stood and went over to the fireplace. The embers snapped and popped as though triggered by his approach. He chuckled to himself at the enormity of the risks taken by the RLA, and that it had all come off. Rhuzkoi joined him.

They accepted another drink from a passing waiter's tray.

"Here's mud in your in your eye!" he toasted the Major, and then added, "and yes, take a break Valentin ... go and do some farming, but not for too long. Get yourself a farm manager, I have some more news that might keep you interested in more covert activities."

Rhuzkoi laughed, "Hah! You Americans ... always playing at spies."

"And baseball – don't forget *why* we're playing spies."

"Ah, yes, I remember you told me – stop all the wars so you can beat everyone at sport."

"You got it, brother."

The waiter retrieved the empty glasses from the mantle above the fireplace, then nodded to signify another round was on the way. It was now dark outside.

"And your news? Something that is more important than growing the potatoes to make more vodka?"

Blackett grew serious again, "At the request of General Vlasov, our OSS has been assisting with an investigation into the deaths of several senior Soviet military officials."

"Oh? Who were they?" Rhuzkoi asked with only minimal interest. He knew there had been a bloody purge at the top ranks of the Kremlin as defeat had become inevitable.

"Military intelligence mostly, some NKVD officers ... we think they just knew too much."

"Knew *what* exactly?"

"Information about weapons," Blackett said matter of factly, watching his counterpart's face for a sign that he knew anything. There was none, and he continued.

"Specifically, technology captured from the Nazis, jet engines, rockets, tanks ... quite an arsenal."

"*Oh Boze moi*, I need another drink."

Blackett smiled, his fish was hooked, now to reel him in.

"The trail of dead officers leads right to the top, to Stalin's doorstep."

"Don't worry," said Rhuzkoi intently, "we'll find him."

"Sure you will ... and with our help. Do you want to join us?"

"Where are we going?"

"East."

∞

New York Times
March 20th, 1947

"STALIN FOUND"

Unconfirmed reports from Moscow describe the burnt remains of a body found in a crashed transport plane several hundred miles east of the capital as "almost certainly being those of the Soviet dictator."

There is speculation over the identity due to the incompleteness of the remains. This has been attributed to the activity of wolves in the area. As a result, identification by dental records will not be possible. A press release from the provisional government states

"... that the documents accompanying the body, in addition to the physical features which match those of the former Chairman, have led to our confirming 'beyond reasonable doubt' that the remains are those of Joseph Stalin."

**COSMIC
EGG
BOOKS**

FANTASY, SCI-FI, HORROR & PARANORMAL

If you prefer to spend your nights with Vampires and Werewolves
rather than the mundane then we publish the books for you. If
your preference is for Dragons and Faeries or Angels and Demons
– we should be your first stop. Perhaps your perfect partner has
artificial skin or comes from another planet – step right this way.
If your passion is Fantasy (including magical realism and spiritual
fantasy), Metaphysical Cosmology, Horror or Science Fiction
(including Steampunk), Cosmic Egg books will feed your hunger.
Our curiosity shop contains treasures you will enjoy unearthing.
If you have enjoyed this book, why not tell other readers by
posting a review on your preferred book site. Recent bestsellers
from Cosmic Egg Books are:

The Zombie Rule Book
A Zombie Apocalypse Survival Guide
Tony Newton
The book the living-dead don't want you to have!
Paperback: 978-1-78279-334-2 ebook: 978-1-78279-333-5

Cryptogram
Because the Past is Never Past
Michael Tobert
Welcome to the dystopian world of 2050, where three lovers are
haunted by echoes from eight-hundred years ago.
Paperback: 978-1-78279-681-7 ebook: 978-1-78279-680-0

Purefinder
Ben Gwalchmai
London, 1858. A child is dead; a man is blamed and dragged
through hell in this Dantean tale of loss, mystery and fraternity.
Paperback: 978-1-78279-098-3 ebook: 978-1-78279-097-6

600ppm
A Novel of Climate Change
Clarke W. Owens
Nature is collapsing. The government doesn't want you to know
why. Welcome to 2051 and 600ppm.
Paperback: 978-1-78279-992-4 ebook: 978-1-78279-993-1

Creations
William Mitchell
Earth 2040 is on the brink of disaster. Can Max Lowrie stop the
self-replicating machines before it's too late?
Paperback: 978-1-78279-186-7 ebook: 978-1-78279-161-4

The Gawain Legacy
Jon Mackley
If you try to control every secret, secrets may end up controlling you.
Paperback: 978-1-78279-485-1 ebook: 978-1-78279-484-4

Mirror Image
Beth Murray
When Detective Jack Daniels discovers the journal of female serial killer Sarah he is dragged into a supernatural world, where people's dark sides are not always hidden.
Paperback: 978-1-78279-482-0 ebook: 978-1-78279-481-3

Moon Song
Elen Sentier
Tristan died too soon, Isoldé must bring him back to finish his job... to write the Moon Song.
Paperback: 978-1-78279-807-1 ebook: 978-1-78279-806-4

Perception
Alaric Albertsson
The first ship was sighted over St. Louis...and then St. Louis was gone.
Paperback: 978-1-78279-261-1 ebook: 978-1-78279-262-8

Readers of ebooks can buy or view any of these bestsellers by clicking on the live link in the title. Most titles are published in paperback and as an ebook. Paperbacks are available in traditional bookshops. Both print and ebook formats are available online.

Find more titles and sign up to our readers' newsletter at
http://www.johnhuntpublishing.com/fiction
Follow us on Facebook at https://www.facebook.com/JHPfiction
and Twitter at https://twitter.com/JHPFiction